Gay Like Me

Gay Like Me

A Father Writes to His Son

Richie Jackson

HARPER

An Imprint of HarperCollins*Publishers*

HarperCollins books may be purchased for educational, business, or sales promotional use. For information, please email the Special Markets Department at SPsales@harpercollins.com.

FIRST EDITION

An extension of this copyright page appears on page 163.

Designed by Fritz Metsch

Library of Congress Cataloging-in-Publication Data

Names: Jackson, Richie, 1965–
Title: Gay like me : a father writes to his son / Richie Jackson.
Description: First edition. | New York, NY : Harper, [2020]
Identifiers: LCCN 2019034198 (print) | LCCN 2019034199 (ebook)
    | ISBN 9780062939777 (hardcover) | ISBN 9780062939784
    (trade paperback) | ISBN 9780062939807 (ebook)
Subjects: LCSH: Jackson, Richie, 1965– | Gay men—United
    States. | Fathers and sons—United States. | Gays—Identity. | Gay
    parents—United States. | Parents of gays—United States.
Classification: LCC HQ76.2.U5 J33 2020 (print) | LCC HQ76.2.U5
    (ebook) | DDC 306.76/620973—dc23
LC record available at https://lccn.loc.gov/2019034198
LC ebook record available at https://lccn.loc.gov/2019034199

20 21 22 23 24   LSC   10 9 8 7 6 5 4 3 2 1

For Jackson, because of Jordan.

"We were gay. Now we're human."

—HARVEY FIERSTEIN, *Safe Sex*

Contents

Gay Like Me

My Son

My Son,

The single dream and drive of my life has always been to be a father. I didn't have career goals, never fantasized about money or glory or fame. All I wanted was to catch a ball in the backyard with my son. I didn't desire power; I desired paternity. In 1984, when I was eighteen, I told my mother that I was gay and that I was going to be a father.

I have always felt lucky to be gay. I've known since the third grade that I was gay, and even then it made me feel special, unique, chosen. I still feel that way. It is the blessing of my life. Everything good that has happened to me is because I am gay. Everything I think, believe, crave, create, conquer, comes from being gay. I've marched, stood silent vigil, protested, picketed, boycotted. I have spoken up, spoken out. I have buried friends. I have had relationships, created a family, had that family fractured, then recovered and rebuilt a new one. I am used to the highs, the lows, and the loves. I am familiar with progress and bitter setbacks. I can rejoice in celebrations and navigate danger. But none of this came easy, and the journey to this point was a long and difficult one.

I was seventeen years old when I moved to New York City in 1983 to attend New York University, right in the heart of Greenwich Village, right at the dawn of the AIDS epidemic. The early 1980s were a harrowing time to be gay. The entire world seemed to be lined up against us. A plague was ravaging us, a new group called the Moral Majority was demonizing us, politicians used us as punching bags, and cardinals stigmatized us. There were very few laws to protect gay people. There were no out elected officials. There were no out movie stars; there was no visibility, no representation on TV. It was as if I'd joined a secret society, bound together by oppression, and we reveled in our clandestinity even as we fought to assimilate.

When *Nurse Jackie*, the television series I produced, ended in 2015, I had an idea for another television show that I wanted not only to produce but to create. It would be about the differences between being gay when I was seventeen and what it's like to be gay now. Growing older in the gay community has never been easy, but now there are many of us who find it hard to recognize the community we were born into. So I wrote plotlines to develop the story of how we reconcile our younger and older selves. I created the two primary characters: An older gay man named Guy, newly single at sixty-two, who is a fish out of water in his own community. In my story he finds himself roommates with a young twentysomething gay man named Zack, who is new to New York City. Zack pushes Guy to date and go on Grindr; Guy gets Zack to lift his face out of his phone and teaches him how to street cruise.

Just when I was putting this pitch together, you told Daddy Jordan and me you were gay. Suddenly everything I was trying to make up was real and happening right at the dinner table. You and I stood looking at each other across that complicated divide. And now you are eighteen and going off to college, and suddenly it doesn't feel like just a comedy anymore. It's a drama with high stakes. Now I write to you as a fellow member of the grand LGBTQ community in which we are both a part, as gay man to gay man.

DADDY JORDAN WASN'T in our lives when you were born. It was ten years into my relationship with BD when he and I had the life-changing conversation about having a baby. Sitting on the deck of a house on Fire Island, having just returned from a family reunion with our parents and our nieces and nephews, we felt the strong pull to start our journey to making our own family.

When we were pregnant with you and your identical twin, I was in a state of elation and agitation. I was thrilled but petrified that something would go wrong. Identical twins—I can still remember all the joyful faces of the people when we told them we were about to be fathers. The world had spun to a magical new place and it was good, if frightening. Surrogacy and in vitro fertilization were so new, and I was so scared.

On May 28, 2000, the phone rang at 11:30 p.m. I had been asleep for two hours. BD was visiting our surrogate, Shauna, in California. I picked up, and he said he was rushing Shauna to the hospital as a precaution, because she was having contractions. Your due date wasn't for another three months. He said he would call me back and hung up. I waited hours. Finally, BD called: Our babies were born, they were boys, premature and fragile, and our firstborn son had died. We had to quickly name you both, deciding which of the family names we had chosen would be relegated to a grieving memory. Then he said he'd call when he had more news about you and he hung up. I got on the phone with United Airlines to try to get the first flight out in the morning to Modesto.

Your twin brother, our Boaz, died after two short hours of life, and you, at a frail two pounds and thirteen ounces, were battling mightily to hold on to your own life. Your tiny body could fit into the palm of my hand. The first morning I saw you, the doctor told me that you would likely not make it, that you would probably die. I was sick with worry for you and I mourned. I mourned your brother, mourned all that you had already lost, and I mourned my shattered expectations. I understand now that the reason it's called "expecting" when you are pregnant isn't only because you are expecting a baby; it's that the minute you hear the news, your expectations of what your child will be and of what your life will be instantaneously coalesce. And over the next nine months (or in our case six) you obsess and fantasize and plan for each part of the life you have envisioned.

We had to airlift you to University of California San Francisco Medical Center because it had a neonatal intensive care unit better able to care for you. Your first three months of life were spent in an incubator in the NICU, hooked up to a machine that helped you breathe.

You were prodded and poked. Your tiny veins were so worn from intravenous needles that at one point they had to put an IV line into your head. Every day was an emotional roller coaster with the mounting medical news—he's going to be blind, he's going to be "klutzy," he is going to need an operation.

You were so sick and your life so precarious. At one critical point you needed a blood transfusion. Because BD and I are gay, we were prohibited by US Food and Drug Administration regulations to be your blood donors. We had been parents for just two months; you were lying in an incubator, unable to breathe on your own, hooked up to a dozen wires; and because we were gay we couldn't take care of you the way you needed to be taken care of, the way we had pledged to care for you. As I seethed, a stranger's blood coursed through your veins. Being prevented from giving you our blood wasn't a medical precaution—the doctors and staff knew that we were HIV negative: we had to be tested to do the surrogacy—it was a smackdown. A smackdown when we were already down—one son dead, one son in critical condition who may not survive. We were helpless, and were made to feel even more helpless. We were being locked out as the IV in your tiny arm released that stranger's blood into your system. Just a few months old and you were already confronted with gay prejudice.

Now the FDA requirement is that gay men are not allowed to donate blood unless they have been celibate for twelve months. We are not assessed individually but as a group, and as a group we are labeled a risk. The lifetime ban has ended, but the prejudice that gay men are diseased, unclean, still stands. During catastrophic crises, when the Red Cross sends out those calls for emergency blood donations, our patriotism and volunteerism call us to act, but we are denied.

YOU SURVIVED, AND thrived, and we parented on. We flew back to Manhattan, your every breath aided by an oxygen tank, as we took turns holding you in our arms. Your brother's ashes were in a cardboard box in our carry-on luggage placed under the seat in front of us. Neither of you was ever out of our sight.

* * *

YOUR BIRTH WAS an arduous effort that stretched across our unwelcoming country. In fact, your entry into this world, into this country, to being born an American, was consummated in homophobia. Because we—your "intended parents," as surrogacy terminology calls it— are gay, we had to twist and bend and jump hurdle after hurdle. Even though we lived in New York State, the only way you could be born into legality and legitimacy was in California—2,912 miles away from our home. In 2000, paid surrogacy was not legal in New York State (and disgracefully still isn't; a bill pending in the state legislature could change that), and California was the only state where there was a judge who would allow two men's names to be on the birth certificate. Our caring carrier, an incredible young woman, lived in Modesto, California. Our home, New York City, with the best medical care in the world, was off-limits to us.

Your very existence, your health, your beating heart, your lungs breathing on their own, is a triumph over bigotry. You have shown from when you were a mighty two pounds thirteen ounces that you have true grit. You are joining a great, vibrant community, with many roads and paths ahead of you. The paths you choose and what you do along the way are entirely up to you. To build on the poet Mary Oliver: What is it you plan to do with your one wild and precious *gay* life?

Being Gay Requires Double Vision

I AM SO EXCITED for you—and filled with anxiety—that you are leaving our home to live as a gay man in New York City. High school is over and you are college-bound. You are kind, responsible, and hardworking. You are ready for college—but are you ready to be a gay man living in America?

YOU WERE FIFTEEN when I watched with joy as you began to spend time with another young, free boy. All those first courtship steps, your adolescent fervor, your singular focus, your trying on how to be part of a couple. I was thrilled not only because you had a friend with whom you were partaking of all the teenage rites of passage of first blush, but specifically because the object of your affections was a boy. My greatest wish for you was for you to be gay, for you to have a gay life, for us to have that central part of ourselves in common. Being gay is a gift. It's the world revealing itself in all its glorious otherness, saying go it your own way, make it yours. The revelations are endless. There are no expectations of what you need to be or to do. It is the blankest of canvases. It's freedom. It's the gift of possibility.

I am so happy you are gay. There is so much about being gay that I am eager for you to experience. The amazingly diverse community that you are now a part of and that is now a part of you—the brilliant, funny, creative, inventive, courageous, wicked, strong, heroic lives you are among. The chance to love and to be loved by an extraordinary individual. The creativity that will permeate your day because there is no set course you must follow. I am thrilled for the flight ahead of you; I am wary of the fight ahead of you.

When I rejoiced that you were gay, I was really wishing for the good parts—the community, the camaraderie, the creativity. The incredible beings who populate our community, who against all odds are themselves. But you can't be gay with just the good parts: your life daily will be touched by all the difficult parts too. The fight, the struggle, the challenges, will make it even more valuable, even more worthy. And as you set out on your gay adulthood, I know you have mistakes to make, lessons to learn, and that you will seek your nourishment your own way. As one of the people responsible for bringing you into this world, and for your well-being, I have to share what I know as a gay man, to provide you some tools that I didn't have, and to prepare you for what may lie ahead.

One of the confounding things about being gay in America is what the sociologist W. E. B. Du Bois described as double consciousness. He was referring to black Americans when he wrote: "One ever feels his two-ness,—an American, a Negro; two souls, two thoughts, two unreconciled strivings; two warring ideals in one dark body, whose dogged strength alone keeps it from being torn asunder." You are an American; you do all the things Americans do; you even have the dream. But America doesn't want you, doesn't accept you, is systematically attempting to erase you. Schools don't teach about you; laws don't fully protect you. The America you think you are a part of is a mirage. You must every day keep a certain clarity about yourself yet remain keenly aware of America's vision of you. You need that dogged strength that is partly the spirit of protest and partly the shoring up of your gayness so that your gay line of vision is clear, beautiful, strong. Living as a gay man means holding this double vision, and I have to attempt to show you how to make both your visions strong.

As you prepare to go to college as a gay man facing the world, a gay man in America, it is critical that I tell you everything I know—everything that I have learned, every rise and every depression, so much that I have kept to myself so that you would feel safe. All of that I have to tell you now. How else will you survive? I need to show you how to keep your body safe, your heart strong. I need to get you angry, and even scare you a bit. And though it may seem that I am clipping your wings just as you are about to set off, I am merely watching out for you from my vantage point, ensuring that you take flight safely, to soar freely.

Visibility Is Not a Cure-All

WHEN I LEFT home for college I had no gay self-esteem. I didn't know gay history, hadn't read gay literature, or been exposed to gay culture, and certainly wasn't educated about gay sex. Gay people usually learn these lessons when they first emerge from their family and discover what they need by trial, error, and tribulation. By steeping oneself in our customs, mores, quirks, heroes, and villains, gay becomes your lens, your filter, your identity.

I came to New York City to find my gay life, to matriculate into my gay self from the good Jewish boy I had been up until then. My family didn't have a lot of money; I scooped ice cream all through high school to help pay for college and still needed financial aid, student loans, and a part-time job to get me through. The extraordinary privilege I did start with was having parents who never said a negative word about any group of people. I never thought there was anything wrong with being gay because I grew up in a household without judgment. My parents treated everyone the same and fostered that attitude in me and my siblings, an implicit education that gave me confidence that my feelings and thoughts and ideas were worthy. What I found when I got to the city was revelatory and jarring. I wasn't prepared for how marginalized gay people were. Gay bars had tinted windows so nobody could see inside. When you bought a gay book or magazine it was bagged in discreet brown paper. We were outlaws, renegades, free but oppressed, silenced, scorned, scolded. My coming out wasn't only a culmination of an exploration and an evolution of identity; it was a political act. We had to come out to be counted and force the government to fight AIDS. I joined a community just as it was preparing its own frontal attack in an unfolding war for our lives. My first public acts as a gay man were to attend protests. Being gay and being political have always been intrinsically linked for me.

So much is different now. You are coming out in a world with Marriage Equality, a drug to help prevent HIV (PrEP), and with laws to protect you. There is even an app to locate the closest gay guy to you. Gay people are visible everywhere now—teachers, sitcom stars, Olympians. We are a voting bloc, a marketing demographic. LGBTQ is now PC. The secret club has vanished; the Pride March is now a parade; corporations stand up for gay rights like a conscience on their bottom line. Your gay generation has more clout, more political capital, more powerful allies—companies, elected officials, famous people. You yourself have gay parents, are out at your high school, and are a member of your Gay-Straight Alliance. You have gay teachers who share their coming-out stories with you.

When I asked you if your school had other same-sex families, you said you didn't know—"*That's your issue, not mine,*" you informed me. You accuse me of making everything about being gay; being gay isn't a big deal anymore you say. You see gay couples holding hands on the street—something I never saw when I was eighteen walking around New York City. There are rainbows everywhere—on car bumpers, hung outside businesses that aren't even gay-owned. You stood as best man at my wedding to Jordan, officiated by our cantor, legally and religiously sanctioned.

You were never in a closet; you didn't start your gay life with that prison of secrecy. How different will it be for you that hiding and lying are not your first entrées into gayness? All you kept saying to me is, "*It's no big deal; it's no big deal.*" You know to ask people their preferred pronouns and have taught me that even the word *queer* is now positive. Though, I still do not feel comfortable self-identifying as queer. For too much of my life I have known it to be a painful, derogatory term. As you enter the world through the portal of the gay community, I wish I could just be thankful for the things that are better for you in the year 2020, and rejoice that so much of gay life has come out of the shadows.

The first time I walked in the Gay Pride March in

New York City was in June 1984, and as we neared the end of Fifth Avenue at Washington Square Park, there was a police paddy wagon waiting with its back doors opened. We were seriously scared that we were being led into it, that the parade was just a ruse to round us all up and quarantine us. We marched past protesters with signs that read GOD CREATED ADAM AND EVE, NOT ADAM AND STEVE and SMILE IF YOU HAVE AIDS. Pride was a rebellion, not a logo. Each contingent was a grassroots organization that stood for part of our struggle, banded together, not branded.

Pride is no longer a protest—it's a bandwagon, a cheerful, celebratory parade. Rainbows abound and the colors are blindingly positive. It's more Hallmark than harrowing. Each year we go as a family. We don't march; we just watch, wave, and cheer. We always stand on the same street corner, at Fifth Avenue and Twelfth Street, across from my old college dorm. I recall how we reveled joyously after Marriage Equality as Governor Andrew Cuomo strode past us, and gay elected officials triumphantly forged down the center of New York City. We cheer for the men and women in uniform—police, firefighters, first responders, and veterans. Some of the world's largest corporative brands float by, and we applaud the hordes of their brave out employees as they march to display their pride. I stand in awe and marvel at the marketing of it all. While I am grateful to be watching with my husband and sons, I miss the rage of my generation—and I miss my friends who did not live to take in this moment.

Today corporations court your business; they flex their muscle to fight anti-LGBTQ legislation they deem bad for their image and their employees. I remember when we made it an effort to shop only at gay-owned and -operated stores, and stamped "Gay Money" on our dollars to prove our actual currency, but you take it for granted that you're welcome as a customer every-where. Instagram is a portal for you to see all types of gay lives and identities, the gorgeous kaleidoscope I only ever got to see every year on the last Sunday in June.

Our new mainstream identity, however, is a false salve. The veneer is better but not good enough, and better doesn't mean right or just. Your being "more legal" gives a false sense of security: it doesn't mean you are safe. And the miracle of visibility hasn't made us whole.

We so wanted you to feel safe, and to see our family as just as legitimate as your friends who have a mommy and a daddy, so we shielded you from many of the re-alities we face daily as gay men and as a gay family. As a result, we may have left you ill-equipped to be what you need to be now—an aware, alert, and on-alert gay man. It's time to lift the powerful, impenetrable shield we built around you in order for you to feel safe and risk revealing to you that our family life, which we fought so hard for and nurtured so assiduously, is, in fact, precarious. It breaks my heart to have to share with you the level of hate and animus that your being gay will elicit. It saddens me that I have to show you the violence always lurking and the fierce, angry wave currently corroding and destroying our rights—rights my generation and the generations before me fought for and won, and foolishly thought were settled.

Your confident attitude about being gay when you say your generation just doesn't think it is a "big deal" greatly concerns me. I am afraid that you aren't aware of what it takes to be an out gay man in a society that deems you as less than others, of the fortitude, stamina, and perseverance needed to live a safe, fulfilling, and prideful life of gay self-esteem in a world that is trying to erase you. Yes, this troubles me, and I need to make you understand what is ahead of us.

YOUR GRANDPARENTS RAISED me and my siblings without judgments or prejudices, so I have never thought about being anything other than what I was. I have never wished to be straight, never cared to be like heterosexuals, or fundamentally changed anything about myself to be accepted by them. I have often felt that my life was a spectacle for straights. Like those cavepeople and prehistoric animals behind the dioramas we'd visit at the American Museum of Natural History when you were little, I have been gawked at, examined, studied, admired, and dismissed—*Oh, isn't it just remarkable how those gay people live!* I've often felt like the attraction, the funny, weird alternative to predictable heterosexual lives. Bachelorette parties are ubiquitous at gay piano bars, and straight day-trippers flock to the Invasion of the Pines, Fire Island's annual Fourth of July drag queen event. Even to our enlightened straight friends, we are often cast as the court jesters, the minstrels, the fun gays added into a party like a human trail mix ingredient.

You always accuse me of thinking being gay is better, and I do. You can't one hundred percent claim your place, your spot, seek your life, if you don't deem your very essence worthy. Gay people may be more visible, but the fact remains that the entire scaffolding of America is constructed for straight people. At every turn we are shown and told we are separate, less than the norm. We are susceptible to feeling as though what we are doing isn't legitimate, or if it is, it isn't as real as what straight people are doing.

Daily politics and religion will try to rob you of your humanity, news programs present bigotry as opinion, most TV shows and movies have no trace of you, and newspaper articles are written primarily for and about straight people. We accept not talking about being gay at work for fear of being fired, or not being out at family events so as not to make other people feel uncomfortable or to provoke their hostility. We tolerate anti-gay teachings from our established religions and vote for politicians even when they don't step up to support LGBTQ rights openly, choosing to overlook their flimsy line about evolving on our basic rights. We build our lives alongside people wanting to destroy us. We are told that our basic human desire for love and dignity and our need for safe shelter are provinces of heterosexuals, and we are portrayed as stealing it, co-opting it, ruining it. So it takes purpose, intention, and discipline to live your life against all odds.

Even with all the advancements—Marriage Equality, PrEP, anti-discrimination laws, visibility, increased representation—things are still going to be tough for you. Our recent liberation has also been observed by our adversaries. Anti-LGBTQ organizations, the Trump administration, and the majority of state legislatures have witnessed our liberation too, and are lined up against us to deny us our hard-fought freedoms, our gains won with the loss of lives equivalent to a war, and to not allow us our human rights again.

When my dad found out I was gay, he said to me, "I just don't want you to have such a hard life." Something in me tells me to repeat those words to you. I know it will be harder than you can imagine.

Find and Ignite Your Anger

WE WERE ANGRY. How can you be gay without anger? Sadness and rage were so much a part of my gay awakening, and I've held on to these emotions. Sadness at watching your friends and teachers die, to be afraid to be touched or to feel someone else. Anger that you are being ignored and vilified. When I was at NYU, I was already protesting, fighting for survival. Leave the sadness with me but share my anger. It's still relevant and will be of use to you.

I learned on my first day of being a dad that I can't always protect you, and I am not fooling myself now. Being gay can be treacherous. I don't want to pass down my trauma; I do want a better gay life for you. You think that being gay isn't a big deal. This isn't true: it is a big deal—it's your heart; it's your connection to your fellow travelers; it's who and how you love, how you will be judged, governed, and politicked.

If you don't think being gay is a big deal, then it will be just like an affect or a hobby, and you will be a tourist visiting Gay World—like our visits to Disney World when you were a little boy, a magical place with thrilling rides and funny characters. Being gay is your biggest artery to your young, vulnerable heart, and if you diminish it, neglect it, undervalue it, your heart will break. Have faith in your gayness.

Being gay is not a lifestyle; it's life. My gayness is the most important, best part of me. It is the blessing of my life, and I want that for you. But it takes daily managing, because it can be as much of a challenge as it is a joy.

I can at least try to keep you safe; work to understand your youthful gay life and culture; engage you as an elder, not just as a parent, to make you a good gay citizen; encourage you to employ all your potential and abilities to have a positive gay life and to improve the lives of all others. I can now raise you gay, educate you in gay history, gay sex-ed, gay geography, gay art, and gay culture. I didn't fully educate you in all these areas as you were growing up. I didn't share all the difficulties that I encountered or that our community has faced. I wanted you to feel secure. I wanted you to know that I was strong and would take care of you. When I told you there was nothing to be afraid of, I wasn't being entirely honest.

Coming Out and Joining In

I HAD TO GO to NYU to come out. I had tried to do it twice in high school to little effect. The first person I told I was gay was my music teacher, and she just hugged me and seemed very sad for me. I next came out to my best friend at the time, Alan, who when I told him I was gay just said, "No, you aren't." We never discussed it again.

When I was seventeen years old I got a lifeline from an ally—my mother. She had seen a Broadway show that she loved so much that she bought more tickets on the way out to take me. Going to the theatre was a special treat for our family because of the cost, so her paying to see the same play twice was a rare occasion. She told me it was an amazing play, with an extraordinary performance by the lead actor who was also the playwright. His name was Harvey Fierstein.

I asked her what it was about. She said homosexuality. I was shocked she thought to take me. I was eager to see a show about gay people, but I was certainly apprehensive to go, worried about how gay life would be portrayed on the stage, and how, at that closeted period in my life, that portrayal would reflect on me, especially in front of my own mother.

This groundbreaking play, *Torch Song Trilogy*, is about a man named Arnold—a drag queen—trying to find love and demanding acceptance as a gay man in 1970s New York City. When he does finally find love, his lover is brutally murdered in a gay bashing. Ultimately, he makes a home with the foster child he adopts, and the play culminates in a confrontation with his mother, who has never approved of his life.

At the end of the play, the mother says to her son (played by Harvey) that being gay is a sickness, and that if she knew he was going to turn out gay, she wouldn't have bothered.

Arnold tells her, "There's nothing I need from anyone except for love and respect. Anyone who can't give me those two things has no place in my life. You're my mother. I love you. I do, but . . . if you can't respect me . . . you've got no business being here."

And she leaves.

After the show, my mother said to me, "If you ever came home and said you were gay, I would never react like the mother in the play." It was as if she had said, *I know you are gay and I am helping you come out.* In spite of her gesture, her invitation, I didn't tell her at our dinner afterward. I couldn't adjust to this new information. For so long I had planned exactly how and when I would come out, and even though my mother's prompt was incredibly loving, I couldn't just switch gears that fast. Nevertheless, at the same time an enormous sense of relief and calm washed over me.

The entire day was breathtaking. Harvey Fierstein was a hurricane force on that stage, in his bursting-with-love character Arnold, the first gay adult I had ever encountered. And this character had desires that mirrored my own—to be in love and to be a parent. I was overwhelmed by my mother's gesture. She had no gay friends, no gay coworkers, and virtually nobody in our world was talking about gay people back then. It was her own humanity that got her to use a Broadway play like a crystal ball and show me my future. It showed me a life that could be possible for me. Watching Harvey Fierstein play a gay man wanting to be in love and have a child and forcing the world to come around to him was empowering. And following Harvey's words offstage was even more impactful. I had a gay role model. I am the first generation of gay men who grew up in a world with Harvey's voice in it, the first gay beneficiaries of this mighty and fearless warrior. I finished high school still not out to my parents, but energized and enriched.

I came to New York City looking for the same kind of gay life I saw onstage at the Little Theatre in 1982 (later it was renamed the Helen Hayes Theatre). I wanted a boyfriend, a home, and I wanted to be a father. I vividly remember Harvey's now famous interview with

Barbara Walters on *20/20* when it originally aired in 1983. He told Barbara, "I assume that everyone is gay unless I'm told otherwise." My gay self-esteem was just in the embryo stage, and this was a staggering paradigm shift for me. And when Barbara self-righteously told Harvey she couldn't have done this interview on television a few years earlier, twenty-nine-year-old Harvey said, "You could have done it and you should have done it." How could I be any less brave in my life than he was being on national television? That night Harvey explained to the nation that love, commitment, and family are not heterosexual experiences, not heterosexual words; they are human words, he said, and they belong to all people. This warrior spoke our truth decades before Marriage Equality, decades before *Love Is Love*, decades before #lovewins.

Soon after I got to New York City I went to see *Torch Song Trilogy* again, and I wrote Harvey a letter telling him what his show meant to me and my mom. He wrote me back: "Thank you for writing. I'm so happy for you & your mother. So best of luck in school. And go slow & easy in life. There's a right time for everything."

I found my gay spot. I wasn't like my friends who were out discovering all the underground parts of New York nightlife. Gay theatre, activism, and politics were my gay stripes. I got an internship with the Glines, a gay arts organization that had produced *Torch Song Trilogy* on Broadway and whose charge was to use art

to create positive self-images and dispel negative stereo-
typing. Through the Glines I finally met Harvey, and
we have worked together and been dear friends for more
than thirty years. And while he has played iconic parent
roles on Broadway—Tevye in *Fiddler on the Roof* and
Edna Turnblad in *Hairspray*—he practiced his parenting skills on me. In so many ways Harvey raised me.
He educated me for a life in the theatre. He modeled
being a good gay citizen. And he showed me how to
lead with my heart with purpose.

You know Harvey as our funny lifelong friend with
the unique voice who calls you "Cookie Poo Poo," but
he's also a mighty warrior. Now you see out celebrities
all the time, but Harvey was the very first, and he didn't
become famous then come out; he didn't wait till he
was successful to come out; he didn't wait till he had
fuck-you money. He didn't come out because a tabloid
threatened to write about him. He started out, and nobody had ever done that before. It was Herculean.

It was spring of my freshman year when my mom
asked me when I was going to tell her I am gay. I was
home for Passover and we were standing in the kitchen.
On such a ceremonious holiday, my coming out was
very unceremonial. I said, "I am gay and I am going to
be a father." I asked her not to tell the rest of the family,
that I would tell them in due course. She told my father
anyway. She should have respected my process and let
me tell everyone on my own terms and timetable.

My father was not nearly as accepting as she was and said all the wrong things—hurtful, stereotypical things. He told me it was just a phase and that he sees those men in the city on his way to work, and they all look sad and lonely. As I absorbed the impact of his first reaction, I felt so disoriented: this was not the parent I was used to. I ran crying to my car. My mom ran after me, and we drove around while she tried to calm me down. Later that morning my brother, Mark, called; he was away at Cornell Law School and couldn't make the trip home to celebrate Passover with us. When my mom and I told him what had happened and how my dad had reacted, Mark said, "I'll be right there," and he drove the five hours to be with me and to speak to my dad. My dad tried to peddle the same tired tropes about gay men to my brother, but Mark began the process of disabusing my dad of his stereotypes, sharing with him that he had gay friends—in fact, his roommate was gay. After Mark's intervention, my dad said to me, "You know I love you," and I said, "Yes, I do," which was true. We didn't discuss it head-on much after that, though I was heartbroken. I was the baby of the family, cute, precocious, and performative. Even though I struggled academically in school, I was always good, always well behaved, and I wasn't used to disappointing my parents or being angry with them. Just as I was trying to find my footing as a gay man, I felt unbalanced by the first fissure with my parents. My foundation was suddenly shaky.

A couple of years later, my sister Sue was getting married. My dad would not allow me to bring my boyfriend to her wedding, and as accepting of me as my mom and Sue were, they went along with my dad and counseled me to "let it go." It felt as if I were being told by my family to get back into the closet for the duration of the wedding. Just a few months later, friends of my family were married, and we were all invited, including my boyfriend. We rented tuxedos and attended the wedding, along with the rest of my family. As excited as I was for my first invitation as a couple, it was a sad, hollow victory. I was still upset that my own family did not extend to me the same respect that our friends did, that my hurt could just easily be "let go."

I made a list of the high school friends I wanted to come out to, and one by one I took them to the diner, our old hangout, to have the talk. My friend Matt shared the news with his mom and she told him to stay away from me. Another friend started to tell people that I had come on to him while we were in high school, which was untrue.

This was the beginning of my adjusting to the split screen so prevalent in our community—my burgeoning, confident gay self on the one side and the negative perceptions from my family and old friends on the other. It was the first time for me that I didn't feel integrated: I couldn't continue on my gay trajectory and at the same time see myself as a disappointing son or a friend to be avoided. I had no intention of cutting anyone out of my life and knew it would take work to adjust all the wrongheaded ideas that were being thrown at me. But in the meantime, I hit the gas on NYU and New York City gay life, and left Bellmore, parental disapproval, and high school in my rearview mirror.

WHEN I STARTED at NYU I finally met other gay young men. We were all new to the city, new to being gay. I had left my safe, stifling Long Island town, moved out of my parents' house, and cast off the constraints, but I didn't know how to be, live, or love gay. We experimented with each other, discovered who we were and what we wanted together. We went to sex clubs, marches, ACT UP meetings. We lived together, nursed each other through breakups and hangovers, had three-ways with one another. We supported each other through coming out to family. We all made mistakes and went down treacherous roads. These were the first friendships in my life that I didn't edit out parts of myself from. We were each other's haven. We had trysts and fights. We were quippy and comfy with one another. We learned gay sex-ed together. We shared dorm rooms and crabs. We moved to our first apartments together. My new friends partied and went out, listened to all the right music, danced at the right clubs at the right time, and worshiped divas, none of which interested me. At night, after all my friends went out dancing or to the bars, timing the taking of their hallucinogenic mushrooms so they kicked in at the optimum moment, I plopped myself on the one armchair in my room, pulled it to the window, and stared out into the forbidding New York City sky. I was alone, my new friends all having a fab gay life that didn't fit me well. So many lonely nights I spent staring out the window of my dorm room. I was finally being who I was in a new place, part of me evolving and part of me dissolving. I was connected to my old self but changing, morphing, deepening. It felt like I had a clear destination—a target, a goal, a destiny.

Even though I didn't have much in common with many of them, we loved each other, and we made for ourselves our first chosen family. We all experienced what it was to be gay together, and now decades later our lives have evolved and track the shared history with so many gay men our age—marriage, children, recovery, HIV long-term survivors, and AIDS-related deaths.

A group of gay friends—bonded—is a pillar of gay life. I know you think that friendships with people who share your interests are all you want. I urge you to gift yourself a gay group. This is the group whom you will draw from, who will draw from you, and together you will partake of all manner of gay adventures. Find joy in creating your chosen family; they will hopefully become your lifelong treasures.

Parenting Is a Marathon, Not a Sprint

I HAD ALWAYS HAD a specific idea of what fathers do, but my dad didn't fit my ideal. He wasn't like my friends' dads or like any of the dads on TV. My dad didn't teach me to throw a ball; my brother did. He didn't teach me to ride a bike or to drive a car; my mother did.

"Cat's in the Cradle," by the famed folk singer Harry Chapin, was my lament:

> *My son turned ten just the other day*
> *He said, "Thanks for the ball, Dad, come on let's play*
> *Can you teach me to throw," I said, "Not today*
> *I got a lot do," he said, "That's okay"*
> *And he walked away but his smile never dimmed*
> *And said, "I'm gonna be like him, yeah*
> *You know I'm gonna be like him"*

The deprivation I felt from lack of playtime with my dad was so intense that once I went up to his study and literally dragged him by the arm to come out and throw a baseball with me. I even devised a special father-son day and nagged him till he agreed to set aside some time for the two of us to spend together. My big plan was to have lunch and go see a movie, something we had never done. The movie my dad chose was *The Odessa File*, a thriller about a Nazi hunter. Even though the movie wasn't remotely appropriate fare for a nine-year-old, I didn't care—it was a fantastic day.

I never allowed that in my dad's silences or those times when he was too busy in his study that maybe he was stressed about money and figuring out how to make ends meet. My dad served on our local school board for ten years, and the nights away at meetings didn't read to me at the time like the civic-minded, engaged community member who he was; it was just another thing that took his time away from me.

Up until the morning after I had come out, when my dad reassuringly told me he loved me, he had never explicitly told me he did. His generation's reserve inadvertently deprived me of his being able to express his love freely. My innate response to that reserve is to tell you that I love you every day, multiple times a day.

My dad's first reaction to my being gay lasted several years. I wish I knew then it would only be his first reaction. We never again had a direct conversation about my being gay, but now he knew a real gay man—not an idea of one, not what he had been taught to think about gay men—and this one he loved. Over time he got more accepting of it and more comfortable. When BD and I started our courtship, Dad had a front-row seat to a gay relationship at every holiday and each family dinner. We melted away that notion my dad had that all gay guys are sad and lonely.

Ultimately, though, my dad's true character kicked in. His moral fiber is stronger than anyone's I know, and his innate kindness got the better of his discomforting prejudice. Today he is deeply proud of my life, of my marriage, and of our family.

Even though we only ever had one quick baseball catch, the benefits of his parenting style became evident to me as I got older, and especially when I became a father. He was simply being himself. While I wanted a buddy, he was stealthily building my character. My dad taught me three things about being a man—be kind, be good, be responsible—and he didn't actually sit to teach me and to talk of these ethics as much as he himself modeled them.

I did have expectations of throwing a ball with you, of teaching you sports and how to ride a bike, but Dad helped me to see the bigger parenting picture that I needed to learn: that by modeling the larger values and morals that he wanted for me, I would then pass them on to you.

The song had it right: I had grown up, thankfully, just like him.

WHEN WE WERE expecting, several of our gay and straight friends thought we were condemning you to a lifetime of being bullied. What would other kids say when they found out you had gay parents? Others commented that we were just trying to be like straight people. Not having kids was one of the perks of being gay, they joked.

While BD and I were trying to prepare for your arrival, we didn't know any gay parents, and we didn't know anyone who had gone through surrogacy. I called the one gay dad I knew of—he was a high-powered, respected talent agent—and I asked to see him. I went up to his agency in a towering midtown building. I was brought into his office, which was entirely dark except for one small desk lamp. I could barely see him through the haze of smoke from the cigarette he was smoking. As BD and I embarked on this monumental life journey, I had hoped for a morsel of wisdom from an elder. I imagined that once we had a baby we would join a community previously hidden to us, an unseen group of gay men who had playdates and family vacations and tips to share. I didn't get any of that. The meeting was very short, and all that this distinguished man said to me was, "How are you going to explain to your child that you paid for them?"

He and his partner had adopted a child, and his view was that adoption was the only way that gay men should create families. He thought that our going the route of paid surrogacy meant that our interest in parenting was somehow consumerist—akin to buying a fancy car or a country house, with the baby as an accompanying luxury accoutrement. It was my first whiff of the divide between those LGBTQ parents who adopt or foster and those who have families through surrogacy.

I am agnostic as to how people build their families. All of us have varying priorities, needs, and capacities, and should be free to go the route of our choice. Paid surrogacy is prohibitively expensive, and I do worry that it creates a caste system among gay parents—that how you create your family is based on your ability to pay. The incredible Family Equality's Path2Parenthood is an indispensable resource and support for LGBTQ people forming families in whatever way suits them best—foster care, adoption, or surrogacy.

You are eighteen and have never suggested or hinted that you felt "purchased." Instead, you marveled at the generosity of my sister Sue, who donated her egg, and our amazing surrogate, Shauna, each of whom were instrumental to your birth and wanted us to be a family as much as we did.

THE GREAT, GOOD fortune of going to New York University Tisch School of the Arts was its vibrant, creative atmosphere teeming with young gay people. It was the first gay community I was a part of, and its elastic bounds of sexuality and gender gifted me a wide, diverse view of humanity. And Manhattan, where I have lived for thirty-six years, is more often than not the progressive port in the stormy sea to shining sea.

Jordan and I are committed to our enormous responsibility and to using our visibility and financial means to support LGBTQ organizations, particularly those for LGBTQ youth who don't have our advantages. When I met Jordan he was on the board of the Gay Men's Health Crisis (GMHC), Broadway Cares/Equity Fights AIDS, and Freedom to Marry. He was as socially engaged and as active as I was. We cannot rest on the glory of our being legally married. It's not our ball to leave the playground with.

Your head start was being born into a prominent family with gay parents, while most gay people are minorities in their own families. You've had the benefit of not being in a closet, and of growing up with and around many positive gay role models. But our privilege isn't a fortress; it is not impenetrable. Nor is it a high ground to stay safe and tucked away in—and certainly not a perch from which to look down.

You are in every way better than I ever was. You are way more interesting, complex, and creative. You have always been a deep thinker, demonstrably self-assured, and, miraculously, you don't have people-pleasing instincts. Even when you were a young child, you never looked for our approval. You'd be drawing in your room, and when you were done, you'd simply put what you made in your drawer. I, conversely, would waste no time to run to my parents to show them, and just hope that my art would get taped to the refrigerator.

I have been amazed over the years at your keen insights and wicked humor. When you were four years old, your teacher asked you what you thought your parents did while you were in school, and you cleverly quipped, "Nothing they are supposed to be doing."

You have always gently guided us on how you wanted to be parented. You were five when I told you not to do something that you found self-soothing, and you rightfully said to me, *"Your job is to take care of me, not control me,"* and when I would tell you to brush your teeth, you'd say, *"Don't tell me what to do; tell me what needs to be done."* These lessons were insightful. You understood what parenting should be and intuitively pushed back against being controlled. You understood early that being ordered to do a task was very different than being asked to participate in what needed to be accomplished. You advocated for yourself by helping us talk to you in the way you knew you'd hear best. Having shown us how to treat you bodes well for how you will behave in adult relationships. I am confident that you will make sure you are treated the way you deserve to be treated.

Your care was out of our hands for so much of your beginning. Neither of us carried you, and when you were born we couldn't start taking care of you until your fourth month. It was on the flight home, and you were four pounds four ounces, hooked up to the plane's oxygen, when, for the first time, we were your primary caregivers. Your whole life I have always had a feeling that I needed to make up for lost time. To this day I know I hug you a little too long, as if you can still slip away. Occasionally now when we are walking down the street or sitting at dinner, you will forget you're eighteen and take hold of my hand—and I am as planted on the ground and as whole as I ever feel.

Complicated/Worth It

M Y ROOMMATE AND I moved out of our dorm and into an apartment on West Tenth Street in the West Village. Now I was in the thick of it—Julius', one of NYC's oldest gay bars, was across the street, and just a few doors down was the quintessential NYC bookstore, Three Lives and Company, which I practically lived in back then and still frequent today. Just around the corner was the Oscar Wilde Memorial Bookshop and Stonewall. I had my first job working on the Broadway shows *Cats*, *Starlight Express*, and *Chess*, and one day I met BD Wong, who had just won a Tony Award for *M. Butterfly*.

BD was unconventional; I was conventional. He was impractical; I was practical. His head was often in the clouds; I was earthbound. Our contradictions complemented each other.

Marriage Equality did not exist and moving in together was unceremonious. When BD and I committed to each other by cohabitating in a loft on Fifty-Fifth Street, we had no ceremony. It was as if we had snuck into our new life in the dead of night and nobody even noticed. The only legal distinction and protection we could invoke was our mortgage status as Joint Tenants with Right of Survivorship. I used to romantically call him my "JTWROS." We lacked crucial standing and community support.

Over the course of the fifteen years BD and I were together, we nearly broke up on a few occasions, but each time we said we couldn't imagine not being together and continued to stick it out. We loved each other, and were compatible, but I think we continually mistook a deep friendship for a relationship.

We had gone to couples therapy to learn to communicate, but we really used it to learn how to break up, and all the while I leaned on my favorite line of poetry from Hart Crane:

> *There is the world dimensional for those untwisted by the love of things irreconcilable.*

Once we separated I never wanted to get back together, and my guess is that he felt the same. There was a lot of happiness during those years, though, and I resisted considering it a failed relationship simply because it came to an end. You don't remember the three of us together. But this separation was the second trauma in your young life. Our charge was to protect you, and we didn't protect you from ourselves. You were two at the time and have endured the burden of our breakup ever since—the bifurcated parenting styles; the dreaded schedule; which house, when? I worried that the concept of home would be elusive to you, that the hearth would have no power if it was dissipated.

BD and I were together since I was twenty-two, just out of college, and then at thirty-seven I was single with a toddler. Because we weren't married we were free to dissolve our union in the manner that best suited us—or, rather, that best suited you. And that is what we tried to do. We took the slow, painful steps of unraveling from each other, each of us dipping our toes into embarking on a new life, independent of the other, but we remained tethered by you. On "hand-off days"—our nonchalant wording for that agonizing moment when one of us would walk away with you—we'd all play together in the park, have lunch, then part ways.

My parenting has irrevocably been altered by your premature birth and the breakup. With each event I felt the ground under me collapse without my being able to stop it. And each time was another uninvited challenge for you.

JORDAN AND I met at the 2003 Tony Awards when you were three. I was there with Harvey, who had been nominated for Best Actor in a Musical for his performance in *Hairspray*, and during a commercial break I went over to introduce myself to Jordan, mentioning a mutual colleague. We spoke briefly and talked about making a plan to have lunch in the casual way most show business conversations end. I couldn't stop staring at him for the rest of the evening, and not just because he's handsome. He was leaning slightly forward in his chair, his chin tilted up, with a warm, open smile, entirely engaged, willing his enthusiasm and encouragement toward the performers onstage. His generosity and kindness were palpable, beaming off him.

I had not been single in fifteen years, and I had to learn how to date all over again. Jordan and I would go to a movie and dinner, and while I would go home and think about my terrific date, it was clear to me that Jordan just thought I was a nice guy in his business whom he was becoming friends with. Finally, after four of these evenings, standing outside his apartment building after I walked him home, I announced that I thought we should date. Jordan said, "It's complicated," and of course I knew what he meant. I was ten years older than him, had just come out of a long-term relationship, and had a three-year-old baby. Jordan was just twenty-seven. I simply replied, "It's worth it." He responded, not unkindly, "It's complicated"— and thus began a thirty-minute back-and-forth that would come to define our relationship. That night I summoned up all the different ways to implore him to take a leap. "It's worth it." "It's complicated." "It's worth it." "It's complicated." After a pensive few moments of silence, he broke the volley and simply asked me, "How would this go? You and I go out, I fall in love with your son, he falls in love with me, and then we break up. Then what?" And with a clarity more level-headed and more direct than I had ever had in my life, I answered, "Why are you thinking of getting out before you get in?" He didn't have an answer for that, and so we began a thoughtful, careful courtship. I pursued Jordan relentlessly. When I dropped him home at the end of the night, I'd ask, "Did you have a good time?" He'd say yes. I'd ask, "Do you want to do it again?" He'd say yes. I told him not to think beyond that. That's all he needed to know at the moment. I would make sure that the following day after each of our sweet, chaste dates, I would send him a poem I wrote for him, or a gift that recalled the conversation we'd had on our evening out. It was to let him know that I was listening carefully to everything that he said, and that I cared about his thoughts, and opinions, and what was on his mind.

After seeing a gay film together, egregiously performed by an entire cast of straight actors, I sent him Langston Hughes's poem "Note on Commercial Theatre":

> *You've taken my blues and gone—*
> *You sing 'em on Broadway*
> *And you sing 'em in Hollywood Bowl,*
> *And you mixed 'em up with symphonies*

And you fixed 'em
So they don't sound like me.
Yep, you done taken my blues and gone.

You also took my spirituals and gone.
You put me in Macbeth and Carmen Jones
And all kinds of Swing Mikados
And in everything but what's about me—
But someday somebody'll
Stand up and talk about me,
And write about me—
Black and beautiful—
And sing about me,
And put on plays about me!
I'll reckon it'll be
Me myself!

Yes, it'll be me.

Jordan and I always tell the story that it was he who took the leap of faith, and rightfully celebrate that he had the courage to let himself be vulnerable in a potentially fraught situation. But I too took a leap. As wounded as I was from the deterioration of my relationship with BD, I staked everything and went all in. It would have been much easier to hold back from a new, serious relationship, but Jordan was too precious and unique, and I realized my feelings gave me no choice.

Jordan is what F. Scott Fitzgerald describes as "possessed by intense life." He is gloriously in his body and in his spirit. His actions are both physical, fully animated, and emotional, emanating from deep within him. Watching him dance is like watching a full-on expression of liberation. It's not just that Jordan is intelligent and has a big heart; what is profound about him is that the mind-heart connection is fully engaged in this extraordinary man.

I had the overwhelming feeling whenever I was with Jordan that this was where I was supposed to be. I had thought my life was one thing, but it was really meant to be here with Jordan. We courted cautiously, and in time we formed our own family.

For my birthday a few months after we started dating, Jordan gave me a needlepoint pillow with WORTH IT stitched on one side and COMPLICATED on the other. When I opened it he said, "I love you." "I love you too," I said.

The next day I sent him Walt Whitman's poem "We Two Boys Together Clinging":

We two boys together clinging,
One the other never leaving,
Up and down the roads going, North and South
    excursions making,
Power enjoying, elbows stretching, fingers clutching,
Arm'd and fearless, eating, drinking, sleeping, loving,

No law less than ourselves owning, sailing, soldiering,
thieving, threatening,
Misers, menials, priests alarming, air breathing,
*   water drinking, on the turf or the sea-beach*
*   dancing,*
Cities wrenching, ease scorning, statutes mocking,
*   feebleness chasing,*
Fulfilling our foray.

Jordan added something to my life that I hadn't aspired to having: being loved. Loving Jordan is thrilling; being loved by him has changed me. Jordan is thoughtful and thought-provoking. He is inspiring and inspired. He's passionate and deeply compassionate. Yes, he is dreamy, but what I love most is that he's a dreamer.

Jordan thinks I can do anything, and he has set out for sixteen years to make me believe I can. When you are loved like that you take risks and have adventures. I came alive. So many of us when we have an idea of something we'd like to do, immediately think of all the reasons we can't do it, shouldn't do it, don't know how to do it, don't deserve to do it, aren't good enough to do it. And the miraculous thing that Jordan's belief in me has done was to erase my pause.

And our growth into a family wasn't nearly as complicated as Jordan feared.

After a year or so of our being together, you on your

own started to call him "Jordan Daddy," and then you morphed that into "Daddy Jordan." We have eschewed the word *stepparent*—no qualifier, no line drawn, no difference, no less than. I feel intensely happy when I sit at our dinner table watching you both make each other laugh. The trauma of your birth is ever present for me, and to see you laugh and eat with gusto brings me such joy, and even now a deep sense of relief.

I NEVER IMAGINED being legally married. My goal was to love someone, but Marriage Equality was unimaginable.

Going to the weddings of our straight friends always depressed me. The deprivation I felt by being denied this rite of passage and disallowed the right to marry brought on a festering resentment. Each time, just as the bride and groom said "I do," Jordan and I would whisper sweetly into each other's ears, "I do."

In 2005 I went to Jordan's father's office not to ask permission to propose to Jordan but to ask for his blessing to join the family. He was very kind and welcoming, and gave his blessing. I proposed to Jordan on his birthday at a romantic dinner—and then we waited seven years until marriage became legal in New York. We wanted to do it officially, legally, in our home state.

On September 8, 2012, we were married. You were twelve, standing with us as our best man, but you weren't convinced it all was necessary. Leading up to our big day you kept asking us, *"Why are you getting married? Nothing is going to be different. You love each other, you love me, and I love you."*

There's so much that made having a wedding special for us. Perhaps paramount was that it afforded us the extraordinary opportunity to express our love, to make vows to each other, in front of our family, and our family of friends. We were married on the stage of the Al Hirschfeld Theatre, one of Jordan's Broadway theatres. It was a fitting venue for both of us: For Jordan, because of his work; and for me, because it was at a theatre in 1982 that I first realized that one day I could be married and be a parent. And our having a big wedding was important to us: we had waited so long, and this was an opportunity to celebrate with so many people from different aspects and phases of our lives.

We enacted rituals that had been performed by our parents, grandparents, and great-grandparents. We used objects from our childhood in the service—the kiddush cup from my bar mitzvah, the tallit from Jordan's. These symbols took on renewed life and meaning as they grew with us into this most sacred moment.

And just as I did when I stood in front of Jordan's apartment to make a case for our being together, again, just as clearly and purely, I said:

"I, Richie, take you, Jordan, to be my lawfully wedded husband. I make this solemn vow in front of God, our family, and our family of friends. With all my heart, mind, and soul, I pledge to expand the canvas of our lives. Walking together, laughing or crying, we will unravel this complicated world together, making the journey for each other safe and always worth it. I choose you to be the person I will spend my life with."

(See how we got "complicated/worth it" in there?)

And when Cantor Sheera Ben-David declared, "By the power vested in me by the State of New York, I now pronounce you, Jordan, and you, Richie—married," my life flashed before my eyes—not just my life but the life of the gay community: the long history of invisibility, the seemingly iron closet, the violence, the bullying, the plague, the heroes, the marches, the artists, the pioneers, the brave, the fallen—all right there with me and Jordan. At the same time I recognized that our new license couldn't wash away all those elements that defined us for so long as gay. And I didn't want them washed away. In fact, that night I also made a covenant to our community, to all my friends who died, to all the long-term survivors—to keep telling our story, to share our history, and never to be silent. Jordan and

I would not be married were it not for everything and everyone who came before us. There would be no Marriage Equality had AIDS not happened. We are the beneficiaries of the sad reality that AIDS brought so many of us out of the closet sooner than we might have planned, that the plague was the tragic icebreaker that slowly started to bend hearts and minds our way. And the political savvy and power that we created and harnessed in the 1980s was brought to bear to marriage. Silence = Death led to #lovewins. It wasn't a quid pro quo, not a fair trade, and I would willingly, voluntarily, hand in my ring to bring everyone back. So marriage isn't a small thing. It's not a pretty, shiny trinket to trot out for special occasions. Its weight, its significance, is both personal and political. It's heart and history. It's intimate and communal.

Everything changed for us when we got married. You changed too. It was immediate, even if nearly imperceptible. The very next day, Jordan and I noticed at the same time that you were magically more grounded, your feet firmly planted in a way they hadn't been before. You had finally found your spot. It was clear to us that your seeing us married, watching it all unfold in a very official, very religious ceremony, gave you a defined family in a way you didn't even know you needed. Daddy Jordan and I felt different too the moment the ceremony was over. We each broke a glass, an expansion of the Jewish tradition, and passionately, triumphantly, kissed in front of our six hundred guests. We felt elevated, lifted up not just by the chairs during the horah, but by custom, by law, buoyed by our guests, sanctified, celebrated, and codified. We too took root in a new, deeper way.

My love affair with Jordan has always felt large and passionate, and marriage gave it new import. It was partly the piece of paper so many people dismiss. After years and years of being on the outside—being told we are less than a full citizen—being sanctioned by the State was healing. To vow publicly, to promise purposefully, our rallying cry to our future and have witnesses support that vision placed us firmly in a tradition in a way that we had never experienced before. Now we had a community of people who wanted our relationship to succeed, who wanted for us what we wanted for ourselves.

There is no underestimating the value of the word *husband*. It is easily understood without ambiguity, clearly defining and revealing the nature of our relationship. The word itself is an equalizer, universal, unable to be diminished. I mean *husband* exactly the same way straight people do.

Young people who are born into a country with Marriage Equality, who know their love and future relationships are valued equally by their government, are extraordinarily lucky. Even for those who don't want marriage for themselves, when their families and houses of worship may demean them, they can point to marriage and say our relationships are equal.

So much of our wedding was triumphant. We had guests from all parts of our family, our family of friends, and our colleagues. Among them were Larry Kramer and, of course, Harvey. We could never have gotten to be grooms were it not for these two legendary gay icons. It literally felt like we were standing on their shoulders as if at the top of a wedding cake.

Our wedding also has a unique distinction, one that is a disturbing reminder for continued fidelity to all LGBTQ causes. One of the guests at our wedding was Donald Trump, along with Melania, and Ivanka and Jared Kushner. Donald Trump is an old friend of Daddy Jordan's father. Pop, Trump, and Jared have business together.

Donald Trump sat right up front as Jordan and I toasted each other and expressed our mutual love.

Melania tweeted out: Congratulations @jordan_roth and @richie_jackson on a beautiful wedding! @realDonaldTrump and I adore u both!

Afterward we received a note from Donald: "Your wedding was one of the most beautiful I have ever attended, perhaps excluding my own (although I am not sure of that)." Then just four years later he blew on the embers of homophobia, transphobia, racism, Islamophobia, xenophobia, and anti-Semitism, and through the glowing ashes rose to be president of the United States of America, taking with him to Washington gay-hating Mike Pence, Jeff Sessions, and Betsy DeVos—all three more of a real and present threat to you than either ISIS or North Korea.

We intended our wedding to be romantic, but every same-sex wedding is inherently political too. Neither of us said anything political however; there were no slogans uttered. Instead, the most radical declaration came from Cantor Ben-David when she started our ceremony:

> "In Hebrew there is not an exact equivalent to the word *marriage*; rather, we use the word *kedoshim*, which comes from the root *holy*. Our tradition teaches that holiness is the way we distinguish something sacred from that which is ordinary. You, Richie and Jordan, have taken each other as individuals but together you make a sacred union of one. You have raised your relationship to a holy place before God."

I hope our nuptials changed some hearts and minds, but that savvy positive approach that many of our civil rights organizations have employed so successfully has its limits. And this period we are in now demands we be more aggressive and confrontational.

DURING THE POISONOUS presidential campaign of 2016, Jordan and I were in the midst of expanding our family. It seemed like a lousy time to bring a baby into the world just as our country's hate and rage were again roiling. But then I realized that the greatest form of resistance is parenting. Raising children is the most hopeful act to change the world.

Over the years Jordan and I wanted to have a baby, and I badly wanted for you to have a sibling. A few years ago we set out on our own surrogacy adventure, and as paid surrogacy was still not legal in New York, once more I had to leave my home state to have a baby. I put to use lessons I had learned, and over the sixteen years the science has improved as well, and more states now allow same-sex couples to be on birth certificates. We wanted a surrogate who was on the East Coast, so that we could attend important doctor appointments and if there were an emergency we could get there quickly. We wanted a carrier who had done it successfully before, and a clinic and a fertility doctor close to home. This time we used an agency called Reproductive Possibilities, and they found us an extraordinary carrier in Virginia. When we talked to Cindy for the first time, she told us she had two children of her own, had previously been a carrier for a straight couple, and each time she had to have her labor induced. She had never spontaneously gone into labor. She joked that she had no eject button. *Perfect*, I thought, and when I told her your birth story, she lovingly, confidently, promised, "I'll get you to the finish line."

She was to be induced the day before her due date. We were having a boy.

We flew to Virginia with you and Jordan's and my parents. And after a long wait and a slow drip of Pitocin, the doctor said, "It's time. Who is catching the baby?" My hand bolted up. I had never volunteered for anything along these lines, certainly nothing medical, and Jordan asked me, "Are you sure? You can't change your mind in the middle." The birth plan arranged with Cindy in advance had been for us to stand by her head, next to her husband, and when our baby was born the doctor would hand him to Jordan for immediate skin-to-skin parent-child bonding. Instead, we all quickly and enthusiastically agreed to change the plan. I put on a surgical mask, gloves, and gown. Our kind obstetrician instructed us that when we see the crown of his head, to reach in under the baby's arms and pull him out. Daddy Jordan and I were holding each other and crying, and when I saw the crown of your brother's head, I pulled him into this world and placed him in Daddy Jordan's arms.

I uncharacteristically volunteered because I knew it would be healing for me. Having missed out on being at your birth, I now was afforded a second chance, to actively participate in the birth of my child.

Levi Emmanuel Roth was born on July 23, 2016, at 1:19 a.m., and we became a family of four. I often find myself stepping back and observing you and Daddy Jordan with Levi. Parenting with your spouse is a beautiful, romantic act, and witnessing the blossoming of your brotherly bond has been breathtaking.

Otherness Is a Leg Up to Extraordinary

I AM—EVEN THOUGH I am married with two kids, one going to college and one in nursery school—still very much, and essentially, other. At fifty-three years old my double vision continues to be 20/20. You always accuse me of creating a false world by following so many gay dads on Instagram and living in a gay neighborhood— *"Not everyone is gay,"* you always tell me. And you are right—I look in these places to see more gay people because so much of our lives are in the straight world, and I want our lives to be mirrored back at us.

Your double vision will have you feel that you are a part of this country. Through that one vision you will work, pay taxes, eat in restaurants, go to movies, maybe even raise a family of your own. But the persistent, dominant, first-priority vision is your otherness.

Whether you feel it as acutely as I did, and still do, you are other. And the way to deal with your otherness is not to soften the edges, not to find the ways to fit in or to pass. It is to double down, to exploit and to expose all those parts of you that are other. Those elements of your otherness are your deep well of creativity and divinity. Your answers reside in your singularity and difference. By amplifying your otherness you unlock your promise and potential. It is there that you will find your way of loving and of being loved.

Let your potential be your guide, and mind it tirelessly. If you are tapping into your potential, spending it wisely, you are on the right track. Money, glory, and fame do not measure potential, happiness does. When you are stuck, dissatisfied, frustrated, your potential is your beacon, guiding you toward where you want to be. It will never fail you.

WE AS GAY people have had to highlight our similarities with straight people in order to get what we want politically, but it is even more critical to rejoice in our differences. Art, literature, theatre, and creativity did that for me. It showed me the gay world; it made sense of my feelings—good, bad, and secret. The gay cultural arts placed me not only in a long march; it placed me in the soul of my gayness.

Your otherness breeds empathy, emboldens ideas, and expands boundaries. Your benevolence, your quests, your talents, your vision board for your future—these are some of the very traits that make you unique. What you need to do is to activate them. Build up your resolve to expose your specialness. The way to stoke it is to revel not only in your own otherness, but in the big, wide, diverse community of otherness of which you are now a part.

I found that I didn't yet know the power that my otherness had in store for me. Gay artists and gay writers showed me how to understand it, how to embrace it, and how to transform it into strength. By immersing myself in their words, their colors, and their creations, I saw the beauty of being set apart. They showed me that my own thread of otherness is part of a great expanse of a bright human fabric.

Gay artists for me were a wonder. Keith Haring was color and hope and conscience. Robert Mapplethorpe took our sexual appetites and elevated them to art. I was buoyed by their honesty and unequivocal sexual expression.

Gay theatre is where I found my confidence. Harvey's *Torch Song* and *La Cage aux Folles* revealed a very real but magical world to me. Terrence McNally's *Love! Valour! Compassion!*, which I saw five times!, is the most beautiful, heartful, chosen-family saga. William Finn and James Lapine's *Falsettos* felt like it was written expressly for me, and Tony Kushner's *Angels in America*, which I first saw holding the hand of my friend Sean who was HIV positive, pointed us forward with intelligence and rage, humor and compassion.

To see two men in performance together at the Alvin Ailey American Dance Theater is a celebration of male sensuality, staggeringly attractive and brazenly out of the shadows.

When I read Andrew Holleran's *Dancer from the Dance* I was home. The elegant, poetic prose validated my urges and desires, and was unquestionably life-affirming in my new gay self-sense. It was my very first literary glimpse into the real New York City gay world, the first book I read written for us, about us. I read these words and understood myself better than I had ever before:

> "Isn't it strange that when we fall in love, this great dream we have, this extraordinary disease, the only thing in which either one of us is interested, it's inevitably with some perfectly ordinary drip who for some reason we cannot define is the magic bearer, the magician, the one who brings all this to us. Why?"

There was Edmund White's revelatory *A Boy's Own Story*, the first book I had read about a young gay man near my own age. I was certainly not unique in seeing myself in Andrew Tobias's insightful *The Best Little Boy in the World*, which back then was published under the pseudonym of John Reid. I lost myself in James Baldwin's exquisite *Giovanni's Room*, which my friend Talia had wrapped and gave me as a coming-out present. As time went on I discovered Audre Lorde, Eileen

Myles, Langston Hughes, and many others. Now I look to the Lambda Literary Foundation for new and exciting LGBTQ voices to discover.

These stories and storytellers—authors, poets, musicians, and artists—are readily available and are well worth your time exploring. I look forward to sharing your discoveries with you.

Reading books by gay writers writing about gay people and seeing movies about us will help you claim your space. Like many gay people, I for years have consumed art and literature and pop culture through a dizzying and tiresome act of substitution. The vast majority of it emerges from heterosexual culture: we have to bend or stretch to put ourselves in the story like a puzzle piece that doesn't quite fit.

We rehear each pronoun; we squint just enough to pretend to see two men. At a certain point I stopped trying to worm my way into straight stories. I stopped accepting that universal was enough to get by on. Substitution is not an acceptable paradigm. It places you firmly on a margin. Each place where you look and fail to find yourself reinforces the fact that you don't exist, that you aren't worthy, that you don't belong. To partake in only mainstream entertainment is crippling and damaging. Love songs that don't comfort but isolate; jokes that suppress and stereotype; franchise films that expunge you. Watch the documentary *The Celluloid Closet*, based on the book by Vito Russo, to see what Hollywood's long, lousy, hurtful depiction of LGBTQ people has been.

Culture eases invisibility. We all need our own specificity of storytellers and stories. Intersectionality is one of our strengths, and each specific strand of otherness in our vast community merits its own amplification.

The nourishment, the best of what art can offer you, is found in gay art. Find, seek, and listen to our stories, the works of the others, and consume what fulfills you. Do not accept table scraps.

Never Diminish Your Essence

RECENTLY I WAS talking to a gay male friend of mine about his husband and soon-to-be one-year-old son. We talked about nursery school and sleep schedules, swapped surrogacy stories and shared parenting advice. At one point I asked him how much of his life is gay. As so much of our lives exist in the straight world, I was curious to see how he balanced it. He said, "Most of the time I forget I am gay and it's a relief."

I was so struck that a gay man can so easily forget that he is gay and be happy about it. I assure you no one who sees him and his husband holding hands on the street forgets, or when they take their child to a playground or do pickup and drop-off at school, or when they travel to some other states or foreign countries.

Being gay is the most important thing about me. I have heard all the damaging delusions—gay doesn't define me; gay is just a part of me; I just happen to be gay—these are dismissals, rendering gay as incidental, merely matter-of-fact. These types of devaluations are disguised apologies for who you are, diminishing you bit by bit, robbing you of the full utilization and expression of your self and all that you have to offer. You have to define yourself fully as a gay man.

My dominant trait is my gayness: my being Jewish, American, Caucasian, and middle-aged—those are all farther down my list of identities. For many LGBTQ people, race and religion are equally, or more, important to them. How someone identifies is a personal choice. You are gay and biracial, and neither needs to have primacy over the other. It's up to you. My gayness touches every part of myself and each aspect of my life. It's how I define myself. I organize my life around it, and it informs who I am, how I act, how I react, how I think, how I feel, how I love, how I care. It's my outlook, my station.

Every decision you make needs to support your gayness. Being gay takes fortitude and true grit, and in order to have these superpowers, you have to have gay self-esteem. When being gay is the filter through which you view everything else, the well from which all your emotions, actions, and reactions spring, you will have good gay esteem.

Each day is a conscious effort to block out all the daily reminders that you don't belong, that you don't participate fully. Being gay means living with the tension between the freedom to be outside the line and the rage at not being inside. It's having confidence while remaining in the minority wherever you are. The stamina to be gay is keeping so much at bay while doing the hard work of living. Our government has declared war on us; there are news programs that present bigotry as opinion; the anti-LGBTQ code words *family values* are accepted as a sanctioned sociopolitical agenda; and legitimate American political party platforms are positioned to be either pro or con on our personhood. All this conspires to tell you that what you are is defective. How do you live large in this deluge? Oppression cannot be a gateway to victimhood, and mere tolerance is not adequate. Do not diminish who you are to find some acceptability. Do not connect your self-esteem with acceptance. You cannot make your gay life small so as not to cause a wave. Do not let hate seep into your profile; do not bow out or retreat because the obstacles seem so great.

The way to defend and deflect is to bolster yourself. Don't just live in the straight world even while trying to change it structurally. The way to fortify yourself is to love and to keep your self-love alive and thriving. Your gay self-esteem is all our culture—our history, literature, art, expression, creations. These are our lessons of trial and error and tribulation.

Buttress Yourself with Gay History

I AM ABLE TO define myself as gay—to be emboldened to live my life on my terms, and to ensure the health, safety, and happiness of my cherished family—because of the long, strong line of magical beings who came before me. I need you to know about the gay warriors, heroes, and activists who have paved a trail for us.

Did you know that the gay community has its own pioneer who, much as Rosa Parks did during the civil rights movement, took a single act of defiance and helped to launch gay liberation? His name is Dick Leitsch, and in 1966 he staged a "sip-in," an act of civil disobedience, so that gay customers could be served in a licensed bar, which was then illegal in New York State.

We have trailblazers like Harry Hay, who founded the Mattachine Society, one of the first gay liberation organizations; Frank Kameny, considered to be the "Father of the Gay Rights Movement," who was fired from his government job because of his "suspected homosexuality" (employment discrimination is a battle we are still fighting today) and coined the phrase

"Gay is Good." Kameny joined forces with lesbian hero Barbara Gittings—comparably named the "Mother of the Gay Rights Movement"—and other activists to lobby the American Psychiatric Association to remove its classification of homosexuality as a mental illness from the *Diagnostic and Statistical Manual*. Del Martin and Phyllis Lyon, who were together for fifty-five years, were founding members of the Daughters of Bilitis, the first lesbian social and political organization. Our founding figures include transgender activists Marsha P. Johnson and Sylvia Rivera, who courageously confronted the police and fought back during the historic Stonewall Riots in 1969. Watch the incredible documentary *The Life and Times of Harvey Milk* to learn about one of the first out gay elected officials in the United States and observe for yourself the difference that one person can make on a movement. The historic 1963 March on Washington for Jobs and Freedom, where Martin Luther King Jr. delivered his "I Have a Dream" speech, was organized by Bayard Rustin, a gay black activist. Our Betsy Ross is Gilbert Baker, the gay man who designed our ubiquitous rainbow flag. Larry Kramer is our agitator-in-chief, first cofounding the Gay Men's Health Crisis in 1982 from the living room of his Greenwich Village apartment on Fifth Avenue (GMHC was, at the time, the only organization offering the gay community information on HIV prevention, advocacy, and care). And in 1987, cofounding ACT UP—

the AIDS Coalition to Unleash Power—mobilizing a generation of young men and women across the nation to action. Their guerrilla-like tactics of in-your-face, dramatic protests and striking graphics were, and continue to be, a reflection of the power of positive gay self-esteem. At one of the very first GMHC AIDS Walks in the late 1980s, as New York City mayor Ed Koch attempted to speak, I witnessed Larry courageously stand alone in protest of him and his refusal to address AIDS as a public health crisis.

I know it is hard for you to imagine how destructive your own government can be to your life, and that my fear of our backward slide is hysteria. The US government's initial response to AIDS is a perfect example of this very real danger. President Reagan did not say the word "AIDS" in public until 1985, four years into America's epidemic. Just watch the Academy Award–nominated documentary *How to Survive a Plague* to view how it took citizens, especially the LGBTQ community, to band together to fight AIDS because our local, state, and federal governments were inert. You will learn about Peter Staley, an ACT UP member and founder of the Treatment Action Group, who battled the government and forced it to change the way AIDS drugs were tested and approved so that they were released quicker to those in need. Today he remains a leader, fighting to make PrEP more affordable and more widely available.

It is easy to believe that one of the great defenders of the LGBTQ movement is Justice Anthony Kennedy, who wrote the Supreme Court majority opinions in numerous landmark gay rights rulings, most notably the 2015 decision to establish a constitutional right to same-sex marriage. But decades of activists and activism enabled Kennedy to swing his votes and majority decisions our way. Follow the comprehensive and wildly compelling @lgbt_history on Instagram to learn our true incredible history.

TODAY AN AWARD-WINNING television show boasts the largest cast of transgender actors in a series in television history. The most popular daytime talk show host is a lesbian. Our same-sex unions, for now, are licensed and our voting can be a bloc, and while I fought for all that to be true and am grateful for all you will have to rely on, I do wish you could have experienced, in our friend Harvey's words, "the great chic mysterious underground" that we created for our own civilization.

Everything I wanted was on Christopher Street in New York. I'd shop for clothes at All American Boy, eat dinner at Trilogy, and I'd lose myself in the Oscar Wilde Memorial Bookshop. The entire street was like Willy Wonka's Chocolate Factory—a trove of gay treasures you couldn't find anywhere else. We had our own newspaper, *The Native*, where I first heard about Larry Kramer and read about AIDS. You have seen plays about gay people on Broadway and on Off-Broadway, in schools and in community theatres, but at the time we relied on the Glines, who were the only ones putting on shows about us. When I was eighteen we had to have these things or else we would have been invisible, even to one another.

It is so much easier to meet gay men now that gay bars and gay restaurants aren't as necessary for you as they were for me. Now there are more gay-friendly places than actual gay places. One of the empowering things about going into gay establishments is the experience of being in the majority, which is so rare in our lives. Finally, safe spaces for our public displays of affection. Our breadth is our greatest asset, but you can't observe that on your phone. You must behold this in real life.

Have Sex in the Light

GABRIEL GARCÍA MÁRQUEZ said that everyone has three lives: a private life, a public life, and a secret life. And that has certainly been the case for me.

Your first sexual exploration with another boy was in your bedroom, in our home with our knowledge and consent. Mine were all in secret—in the park down the block from my house, in the basement across the street at our neighbor's, in the backseat of my car. You started in the light; I was in the shadows.

I knew I was attracted to boys since the third grade. My friend Craig was taller than me, confident, and strong. At first I wanted to be him, but then I slowly realized, *No, I don't want to be him; I want to kiss him*. When I was ten and my friend Daniel was nine we would walk to the end of our block to the park, go all the way to the very back, climb behind tall bushes to a small patch of hidden grass, and we would touch each other. We would tug, jerk, pull. Other times we hid in his basement and he'd take me in his mouth, and I had no idea what we were doing. We were too young to ejaculate but old enough to know to hide and keep secret our fondling.

I hadn't read anything about what we were doing in my Judy Blume books or my *Dynamite* magazines.

When I was sixteen I hung out with a twenty-year-old college guy who had been in my sister's high school class. Scott was very funny, neurotic, and was home on vacation. We never said we were gay, but it was obvious to me, to us. He was my introduction to a whole world of gay sensibility: He was obsessed with show business and diva actresses. He'd take me to see movies in New York City the very first day they were released. To this day I remember every frame of *Reds* and *On Golden Pond*. I felt so mature being in New York City, seeing classy motion pictures with what sure felt like a boyfriend. One special day we went to see Katharine Hepburn on Broadway in the play *The West Side Waltz*.

To fool around we would get in my car, drive back to that same park where I first touched a boy, and we'd kiss, crouched in the backseat to make sure no one saw us. He was the first man I *actually* kissed. Even though he was older than me, he was way more squeamish about sex than I was. He called ejaculating "making a mess" and always seemed to want to stop it as it was happening. One afternoon, after one of our fabulous city adventures, we took the train back to Merrick, Long Island, and in his bedroom I gave my first blowjob and had my first ejaculation with another person. As we lay naked next to each other, our cum still on us, he broke up with me. "We shouldn't be doing this," he said.

He thought what we were doing was wrong. My first time naked with a man, the most vulnerable I had ever felt, and his shame about being gay shut us down.

The one positive sexual experience I did have around that time was with my friend Elizabeth. She and I had been planning on going to prom together, and she suggested we have sex before that special night to, in her words, "take the pressure off." Even though I was waiting to come out at NYU, I felt compelled to participate in the high school rituals of prom and losing my virginity. She invited me over to have tea and pound cake with her parents, and afterward, with their full knowledge and consent, we went to her room and tried out the new IUD her mother had bought for her in preparation for college. I wore a blazer, and we sat with her parents talking about college and life goals, then we excused ourselves and went to have sex. What a difference a gender makes.

My first day of college, while moving into my dorm, I met this mesmerizing kid who was wearing a black-and-gold mesh jersey that came down just to his waist, and even when he stood still he seemed to be bouncing. Kevin constantly threw back his head, ran his hand through his hair, and walked as if he was on a perpetual red carpet. He spoke Italian and rolled his own cigarettes, and I was transfixed. We'd visit each other's rooms nightly, furtively touching, brushing up against each other as we talked. One night we sat on his bed, holding hands, and he told me he was straight, then he leaned in and kissed me deeply. That night we didn't so much fool around as devour each other. Just after we orgasmed, he told me that had he not been accepted into our theatre school he would have gone into the priesthood. In spite of the red flag, I fell hard for Kevin, and after two feverish weeks he told me he wasn't gay, ended it with me, and we didn't talk for several years. Later on we reconciled, made out a couple more times, and eventually I found myself driving to Pennsylvania to watch him marry his first wife. As he kissed her in front of the priest, I could feel his tongue in my mouth. His hand had gripped my face just as he was doing now to her. I didn't know which of the three of us I felt more sorry for. I couldn't have known when we were kids that I wouldn't be able to wash away his ideal of what his life should be. I couldn't soothe the terror he felt at his homosexual impulses and his profound self-loathing.

By near the end of my first year of college, I had yet to have a positive, healthy sexual experience with a man. The first two men I was interested in, the first men to trigger my sexual awakening, had pressed their gay shame into me.

A year later I had my first official boyfriend, and I felt saved. John was tall, blond, and handsome, and I believed I became more attractive by association. It was as if we were in a romantic comedy montage: we visited museums, went to the zoo, had leisurely walks in Central Park. I was so thrilled to have a real boyfriend that I ignored his very serious addiction to shopping, never bothering to dissuade him from his steadfast belief that if he purchased the just-right sweater, its power would change his life. And I never complained that even while we had sex pretty regularly it was always in the dark. The lights weren't out because of romance; he simply wouldn't let me see him naked. One night we were having sex, and just as we both finished, he punched me. "What did you do?" he screamed at me. He tried to hurt me because of all the shame he felt having just enjoyed sex with a man. If you're counting, this is now the third time I was naked with a guy, and the third time shame and sex came to me in the same moment.

All these men's shame about being gay emerged during sex, and I was too young and naive to realize it wasn't about me. I took each personally, and while I have never believed being gay was shameful, my relationship to sex, using my body for emotional expression, being vulnerable with another man, was dealt a permanent blow.

During my first semester at NYU, I started to get calls from a teacher at my high school. He must have been about the age I am now, and he had a son and was divorced from his wife. I never took any of his classes but he was the hall monitor during my lunch period, and he would entertain me with stories about New

York City and Greenwich Village, so it made sense to hear from him when I moved here. He asked to take me out to dinner and show me around. I was happy for the connection to home, and better food than what the dining hall served.

After a couple of these meals, he said he could help me out with money if we fooled around. I didn't need the money, really—my parents were able to pay for my meal plan, and I had a part-time job for spending money. But I still did it. I liked the secretiveness; it was familiar. We met up only twice—once I took the train to Long Island to his house and once we met in a seedy motel closer to the train tracks. I used all the money he gave me to buy my roommates and me an answering machine. As much as I enjoyed the attention and was turned on by the illicitness, I ended it because each time he got on top of me, I felt out of my depth—I knew I wasn't supposed to be there.

At the same time, I was having monthly friendly lunches with another former high school teacher of mine. He was beloved, and the funny, chummy adviser to a cool student activities club, of which I was not a member. But when I was living in New York City, he would invite me to meet him at an Italian restaurant by Lincoln Center before he went to see an opera. We always sat at the bar, he'd buy me a bowl of pasta, and he'd have a glass of red wine. We talked about theatre and acting, and I felt very erudite. On a break from school he invited me over to his house for dinner, and over too many cocktails before the meal he kissed me and began to unbutton my pants. I jumped up and had him call me a cab to take me home. Only years later could I take responsibility for going on what had to feel to him like dates. I was getting the attention I wanted and wasn't thinking about his feelings. He was lonely for company, and my eager, reliable, solicitous young self surely conveyed an interest I hadn't intended.

In both these situations I was acting at being an adult long before I was really ready to be one. Neither seemed particularly significant at the time, but in retrospect I have realized their effect on me, like noticing a bruise long after the initial impact that caused it. I absorbed my lessons from my teachers, and transactional sex remained a part of my secret appetite. Both of these men were in the closet—as teachers back then they couldn't be out—and neither partook of any gay activities or had any positive outlets to express their sexuality. I didn't have the faculty to understand that my path didn't have to parallel theirs.

YOU ARE STRONGER than me, more resilient. Sex is a tightrope. You must trust you can be truly exposed and vulnerable. You must also protect yourself. Never take on someone else's emotional baggage. All the politics, advancement, and visibility don't necessarily translate to the personal. Each man you meet and touch and taste may not be as empowered as you, or brought up with the same foundation of pride; he may not be exposed to the gay world yet or particularly politicized. He may even still be in the closet. So behind each kiss, underneath each belt buckle, can be a scared heart, another inexperienced soul yearning to feel whole. You aren't always going to be aware when you start with someone where in his journey he is, especially when you're in college and so young, so empathy and care are required.

You will love and cry over many men, and you need to understand this even if you are too young to be able to do anything about it now: While everyone brings his own unique damage to relationships, with gay men, shame is often at the root of our wounds. And this wound can be a deep and ravenous hole that will swallow you up if you aren't aware it exists and willing to try to help your mate wrestle with it. The men you will care for and love may come to you with harrowing histories of being bullied or abused, of families who rejected them, and of religions that stigmatized them. Be prepared that much of the work and rigor of your relationships may be in trying to soothe the trauma in your mate. You will find that how you treat that person and all the ways you love him will be in direct reaction to that early assault. Don't just love someone your way; love them the way they need to be loved.

AIDS Is Not Over

M Y BRUISING FIRST sexual experiences were compounded by an unrelenting fear of AIDS, which was still new in the early 1980s. So much was unknown about the disease in those days. I got my rules of engagement in 1983 from a new and controversial safe sex pamphlet called "How to Have Sex in an Epidemic: One Approach." The authors were Michael Callen and Richard Berkowitz, with medical and scientific guidance from Dr. Joseph A. Sonnabend. This informative if controversial—again, so little was known about AIDS that the publication was met by some with skepticism, derision, and anger—pamphlet was a clarion call to the gay community to keep ourselves and one another safe. And for me it was the Gay Commandments. Callen and Berkowitz were the first to introduce the revolutionary concept that gay men should use condoms. My sex life was just developing, but I stuck close to those dos and don'ts, and have done so all these years, for better or for worse.

Back when I was living in a dorm, teeming with young, attractive gay men, I trained myself to hold back and not entirely let myself go. My guidebook warned to kiss only with mouth closed or on the body; to always make sure to wash before and immediately after sex; showers were suggested not only as foreplay, but as a discreet way to see your partner in the light, naked, so you could check for lesions, rashes, or abrasions. I bought, as directed, a fingernail scrub to adhere to the rule of scrubbing under your fingernails with anti-bacterial soap after sex. Before I had even begun I was forced to abandon the notion of sexual abandon, some-thing I had looked forward to becoming accustomed to. I was extremely lucky to have learned about safe sex just in time.

I struggled with condoms and lube. The pause that was necessary in the proceedings to remove the con-dom from its packaging, lubricate, and roll it on while maintaining an erection all telegraphed that I was pausing to ward off disease and possible death, to pro-tect myself from this man whom I was now trying to be intimate with. I couldn't shake peril for performance. Alone in my dorm room I would practice using lube and a condom. I would put them on and masturbate, trying to attain a matter-of-factness, to get used to the sensa-tion. I looked to find ways to eroticize these tasks so as not to dispense with them. The common refrains *I don't like condoms* and *Condoms don't feel as good* weren't compelling reasons not to use them. I kept telling myself that this thin sheath of safety was not an impediment to intimacy, just a barrier against fatal illness.

I had been on several dates with Eric, a nice salesclerk from the local Conran's store. One night after a fantastic date we started to fool around, and as things progressed he wanted to have sex, and I said we couldn't because I was out of condoms. He said, "Let's do it anyway," and as alluring as he was, I said no. I wasn't being self-righteous; I was just too scared not to use condoms. He got dressed, left my apartment, and I never heard from him again.

Meanwhile, Jesse Helms, the Reagan Revolutionaries, and Jerry Falwell and his im-Moral Majority were screaming that AIDS was God's wrath on gays. And there was a common saying at the time that when you have sex with someone, you are having sex with everyone they have ever had sex with. As a result, my fear was crippling. I know that because my sexual matriculation coincided with the beginning of the AIDS epidemic, I have been scarred for life, left with the lasting untruth that lingers still: Sex equals death. I have never had sex without the fleeting thought of death racing through my brain—even now, even married. Any cut, sore, abrasion, or birthmark has always startled me, and the fleeting thought of Kaposi sarcoma, a skin cancer affecting people with immune deficiencies, nearly paralyzes me. My flaccidness waved its white flag.

*   *   *

MANY OF MY sexual experiences in college were with friends. We tried, failed, experimented, and learned how to have sex with each other. It was a big, gay playground. In the four years I was in college, I had hooked up with twenty guys. Part of my voraciousness at the beginning was to find guys to affirm what I was feeling and to learn by doing, a chance to pick up a new skill, discover a new stimulating zone, learn a new term. Some of my friends spent time with older men and brought back their findings, adding to our expanding knowledge.

When I sat in health class in my high school, the sex education lessons had no mention of anything about or for me, and to this day LGBTQ students are still not getting sex education that is properly inclusive of their gender identity and sexual orientation. GLSEN (pronounced "Glisten"), a national education organization focused on ensuring safe and affirming schools for LGBTQ students, reports that fewer than 7 percent of LGBTQ students have health classes and sex-ed that include positive representations of LGBTQ-related topics. This lack of information, education, and knowledge is life-threatening. Then there is the systematic erasing of us as we sit in those classrooms. We are implicitly being told that our desires have to be kept in the dark, and that what we are feeling has no value. We aren't taught how to take care of ourselves—or how to care for our partners. Our healthy relationship to sex and to our own sexual identity is thwarted from the point when it's needed most—in adolescence, as growing, developing, curious young LGBTQ people. I would probably not have racked up so many sexual partners so early if I had been better educated.

When you were eleven, Daddy Jordan and I sat down to have the sex talk with you, and we told you about both gay and straight sex because we didn't know how you would identify, and we didn't want to give one primacy over the other. We told you as much as you needed to know at the time, and we hoped we were open, honest, and clear. The absence of LGBTQ history and LGBTQ-inclusive sex education taught in our schools is state-sanctioned. It is no less than systematic and well-regulated child abuse.

Of course, earlier generations didn't have the internet, which makes porn so readily available, as I am sure you know. It may have been helpful to be able to watch videos and get some inkling of what lay ahead for me, but my reality is that I stumbled through so much of my sexual experience. Know this: Porn can be good for some people but it's sport, and it doesn't resemble real life. It dispenses with intimacy and, like the violent video games we didn't allow you to play as a child, is dangerously addictive.

ARMED WITH MY list of safe sex dos and don'ts, I began to seek out dangerous, secret sexual situations in underground sex clubs. Each time I walked down a dark stairwell into a rancid basement, I could feel the conformity of my strict suburban life falling away. I was easing myself into the shadows where I thought gay sex belonged, even though I told myself that this thrilling sexual joyride was a valid expression of gay freedom, a means to deal with the urges in need of a release from our daily life-threatening fears. Even as I was careful and by the book, I resented having to be so constricted. Dipping my toe in illicit (albeit safe) sexual situations was my petulant attempt at rebellion.

As I got older, still living in the shadow of a disease, I always wanted to talk about sex straightaway with my dates or hookups. They would accuse me of killing the spontaneity, of ruining the moment. *Let's just see where things go* was the common refrain. But I believed firmly that in order to be safe, it was important to talk about each act, to agree on what would happen and to settle on what would not. Now this old safe sex rule is called affirmative consent—yes means yes. You too need to talk before you leap so you know in advance your partner's HIV status and they know yours, and if either of you are on PrEP. Agree on condom use if it gets to fucking. I have for years thought I was boring because I am often satisfied with just kissing and jerking off, but that's when I have always felt safest. Yes, the rules I adhered to have kept me safe, and over time I have tried to venture past my self-imposed sexual restrictions, but with little success. Decades later, when Jordan and I first started dating, I was unable to perform. I couldn't deftly handle the lube and the condom without a blazing stop sign of DEATH, AIDS flashing in my head. I was limp with terror.

Anxiety and the rules around safe sex took the sexiness out of intimacy and sowed distrust in my partners. I still had sex, but it was rudimentary, and always careful, always by the book. The checklist of symptoms was continually running through my head; the safety of no-risk activities was my sexual comfort zone. I was never entirely in my body for sex, only ever in my head, and careful never to let go and step over into areas of risky activity.

You can be free from these psychological restraints. You have permission in a way I didn't. Many of the strictures I was ruled by don't apply anymore. You now, miraculously, have PrEP (pre-exposure prophylaxis) to prevent HIV, and PEP (post-exposure prophylaxis), the "morning-after pill," should you be exposed to HIV or think you might have been. Condoms are matter-of-fact for you. You don't have the specter of AIDS hanging over you in the same way I did. You will have much more sexual freedom than I did. The plague that was ravaging the gay community and New York City when I moved here is now, thirty-six years later, a chronic manageable disease (for those with healthcare at least). You don't equate AIDS and sex in the same way that I do. You can experiment and explore men's bodies without the sense of dread and death that always haunted me. But there are still dangers, and without my PTSD, will you have the discipline to be safe all the time?

IT'S HARD FOR me to think about you taking a drug every day so that you can have sex. It's even scarier still to think that you can use an app every day to *find* sex. I have many friends who use both, and it's part of their lives that I hear stories about all the time. I worry that PrEP is making their sexual appetites more dangerous. If I close my eyes as they recount their evenings' exploits, I am transported back to the early '80s— poppers, barebacking, numbering how many men in one evening they had allowed to ejaculate inside them. Risky activities long renounced by my generation have come roaring back.

You know so much more and have so many more options for safe sex than I did, and the fear that has ruled my sex life won't rule yours. But the new safe sex methods and the fact that HIV is a manageable disease are not license to be cavalier. PrEP isn't meant to be a gateway drug to risky sexual behavior. When you become sexually active, you should consider going on PrEP, but always, always, always, combine it with a condom, because PrEP doesn't prevent other sexually transmitted infections. I know that my complicated feelings about PrEP are due to my age and having lived through the AIDS plague, but when we were young we didn't know that HIV was on the horizon for us, and you don't know what could be in store for you. Condoms are the safest way to protect yourself against the unknowns.

Character Counts, Not Profile Stats

ONE OF THE great and challenging things about being a gay man is that sex is available everywhere, anytime you want it. Great because it's thrilling just to be able to hook up with a guy you are attracted to in an unexpected way at an unexpected time in an unexpected place. No matter where you are, if you are around gay men the possibility to hook up is omnipresent. But challenging because sex can be a distraction too. When you can check your phone at any hour to see where the nearest man looking to connect is, sex becomes a self-destructive distraction and can keep you from full engagement at school or at work and in all your relationships.

One of the rites of passage I recall was learning how to street cruise. Partly it was to find sex, but it was also a buzz and an acknowledgment to spot another gay man in public. Now that everyone's staring down into their phones—and those phones can also find you sex—street cruising is nearly gone. It's a titillating, tribal dance that I wish you could have experienced: You'd walk past someone you thought was attractive, lock eyes, and after a few steps, look back to see if he too was looking back, and if so, you two would take a couple more steps, look back again, and then you would stop and he would stop, and one of you would start the walk toward the other. And if you clicked you went directly back to one of your apartments to have sex, and if that wasn't possible you'd exchange numbers. Sometimes the few look-backs without meeting was enough of an ego boost to last the day. This secret frolic is all but gone now.

Hookup apps provide you the opportunity to meet someone easily without leaving the comfort of your home. But recognize there is a game quality to the mindless swiping on cute guys, racking up matches like a scoreboard, and the ease with which you yourself can judge someone else's details. And understand that your being judged on your physical traits and photos may be harmful, in how it makes you feel. Skin color, height, body type, sexual position preference, dick size—all become your currency before your mind and heart. More options may make choosing easier, but it won't make *not* being chosen easier, and treating guys like you are Pac-Man won't satiate any hunger you may have. So much of our own community biases, internal homophobia, and racism are as prevalent in these apps as they were in the personal ads I'd scour in *The Village Voice* when I was in college, with the very specific demands exhibiting some deep prejudices: no fats, no fems, no Asians, straight-acting only.

Hookup apps have also killed mystery and allure. All the naked pictures guys post now—revealing themselves and all their most personal attributes—can be arousing and intriguing, but these enticements leave very little to the imagination. One of the exciting mysteries when you first meet a man is the act of discovery, of removing each other's clothing at your comfortable pace, and learning for yourself what's underneath. All the firsts—the nuzzles leading to a kiss, the closeness giving you a hint of his scent, the exploring of each other's bodies—are what make sex exciting and erotic, and a gift.

We're a people who appreciate beauty and muscular bodies; we're type-focused and gym-obsessed. Don't swim in the shallow end of the gay pool—stay clear of the narcissists. I have never been the "ideal" gay type. This was clear to me when I would go to the bar Uncle Charlie's and no one would look at me, or when I was at sex clubs and everyone would look and walk past me. Now all you need do is look on Instagram at all the gorgeous gay men who post photos of torso after torso, giving the impression that all gay men are hairless; have 6-, 8-, or 10-packs; and enjoy endless leisure time. Scrolling through handsome men can be captivating, but swiping and scrolling will not give you a measure of a man nor will it be a healthy measuring stick for your self-image.

You can have as much safe sex as you want with as many men as you want, but sex as sport does not come without consequences. No-strings-attached sex can be fun but it is not nourishing in the long-term. Hookup culture doesn't allow time to invest in getting to know someone or have him invest in getting to know you. The bait of someone just a swipe away renders everyone easily expendable. Including you.

So much of the centrifugal force of gay life pulls us to parties, clubs, alcohol, and drugs, and to playgrounds like Fire Island, Provincetown, and a long, large popular circuit of theme parties, beautiful men, and pulsing music. If you partake in them, understand that they are like the playgrounds we visited when you were a child. You treat everyone kindly, you always take care of your body, and when you get tired, it's time to go home.

Adolescence is a time of sexual awakening, discovery, and maturation. For those who don't come out during adolescence, we often have to repeat it when we do. So for many of us that kind of emotional tumult and complicated feelings can be happening in our twenties, thirties, forties, fifties, and beyond.

Boy is the cutesy, sexy term gays use to refer to the guys they hook up with or date, or even their group of close friends. No matter what age, or phase of life, everyone is "boy." It sounds fun, frivolous, and mildly rebellious, but it is in fact infantilizing. It keeps us from maturing and prevents us from seeing each other as grown men, and it hinders our developing mature relationships.

ALL THE UNFORCED errors I have made in my life have been around sex. I have been paid for sex and I have paid for sex. I've had sex in tiny booths in the back of X-rated bookstores and was nearly arrested at a sex club that was raided by fire marshals. I've made bad decisions on lonely, horny nights, and nothing I ever found outside alleviated that loneliness. Sex never cured anything. I should have stayed home, jerked off, and just let the moment pass. Do not underestimate the value of masturbation as a savior.

I am so relieved that you have graduated from high school and are not on drugs, but as you join the gay-dating scene, alcohol and drugs will be your third wheel. It is believed that as many as 30 to 40 percent of gay men struggle with substance abuse of some kind compared with 9 percent of the general population. It's a staggering figure, and because addiction is so prevalent in our community, you'll need to safeguard yourself. So much of gay social life includes alcohol and drugs. Bars, clubs, circuit parties, all our events—Pride, conferences, fund-raisers—are brought to you by an official alcohol sponsor; it's wolves in an unguarded sheep pen. Each occasion, no matter how serious, is always followed by a liquor-sponsored after-party. Cocaine, ecstasy, crystal meth, and all other party drugs are dangerously addictive and self-destructive, and even fatal, and while I have never done them, and I like to think you never will, you may find yourself, as I did, in a relationship with someone who is an addict.

I have always avoided drugs and alcohol, because as a gay man I am susceptible to addiction, just as you are. You must be extremely cautious not to fall victim to your predisposition. There are so many reasons for this unfortunate susceptibility of ours: shame, internalized homophobia, damage from our past bullying, immaturity and postponed adolescence, rage at our inequality. Some of us don't come out till our thirties or forties, so there is a compulsion to make up for lost time. For men my age, and what we lived through and witnessed, the unfathomable becomes an understandable factor.

The dad in me wants you to meet a nice guy who treats you well, appreciates how special you are, loves all of you, and likes his own parents. Parental me wants you to settle down early and avoid the chaos and hazards of gay-dating life. But the gay man in me is excited for you to experience your own sexual awakening; to live fully; to have adventures and intrigues; to experiment, explore, and experience; and to blend as best you can your private, public, and secret lives.

Grief Is a Manageable Disease

O N OCTOBER 11, 1987, I went with Harvey to Washington, DC, for the second National March on Washington for Lesbian and Gay Rights and for the unveiling of the NAMES Project Foundation's AIDS Memorial Quilt on the National Mall. Harvey was there to lead the march and to contribute a panel he made for our friend Christopher, who died just three weeks before at age twenty-seven.

It was a beautiful morning, and the Quilt was laid down with elegant choreography timed to each name being read aloud. It covered a space larger than a football field, 1,920 panels snuggly tucked between the very government agencies ignoring us. As we walked on the white paths between the home-sewn panels, all we could hear was sobbing, the names of the dead being read aloud, a mournful elegy. The enormity of the epidemic, the memories of the vibrancy of the lives lost and the creativity extinguished, bore down on us. In so many instances, the men were of my generation. I was also clear about what was irrecoverable for all of us, not just the individual tragedies, but the generation of people vanished—leaders, artists, mentors, educators, parents, poets, prophets. You could see in vivid color the hole that would never be filled. I felt like I was walking along the rows of the Normandy American Cemetery and Memorial. Just like the crosses of the young soldiers there, the Quilt was our brothers and sisters, one after another, row after row.

On three different occasions I went to Washington to march for gay rights. To march in our nation's capital is both moving and infuriating. It was empowering to be in a sea of change agents, signs and banners demanding the way things should be, exercising rights of free speech and assembly. It was also demoralizing to have to walk among the monuments I visited as a child with my family and to now find myself butting up against the same majestic architecture and impenetrable bureaucracy. Each time the AIDS Quilt was displayed, those departed lives were lovingly depicted in a pageant of homemade color, their names echoing out onto the mall in front of the halls of power.

The Quilt cannot be displayed anymore; it's too vast. It now weighs fifty-four tons; there are more than 49,000 panels. The stories of these lives, the neglect that caused so many deaths, cannot be stored away and die out with my generation. I follow @TheAIDSMemorial on Instagram, devoted to telling the stories of these souls. Each post is a loving and detailed remembrance of a person who died of AIDS. The loss is palpable. Inevitably when I see these posts I always think I recognize the people being memorialized, that I knew them. And as I read on and start to learn about their vital lives, I realize I know them because they are us and we are them, an unbreakable bond. This account shores up that bond; its potent hashtag is #whatisremembered-lives.

I want you to start to follow @TheAIDSMemorial. This is not just some parental mandate to know your history. It is for you to absorb the vast, colorful, funny, unique people who briefly lit up our world, to now carry these names and stories along with you, and to celebrate your freedoms. Our family are direct descendants and inheritors of so much of the lives' work of these departed individuals.

I ask you to know the stories of these flashes of life also so you'll understand me better—understand that ghosts occupy a chamber of my heart, that the doom is still so present, and why I hold on to my just-under-the-surface rage. Like a soldier back from war, I kept these battle stories from you. When is a good time to tell your child your story about a plague? I kept putting it off so as not to scare you, so as not to burden you. Nonetheless, as I learned in Hebrew school: Never forget. Never forget that our own government neglected, ignored, and imperiled us. Never forget that it took gay citizens to act up and fight back, and change the course of history. This moment now requires such participation. Never forget that this isn't passive: in fact, it means count me in. You can't be a full participant and leave it to others to fight to make you one. And there will always be LGBTQ people who can't march, who can't protest, who don't live in places where they are safe enough to speak out. We need to speak for them.

While AIDS is abstract for you, I wouldn't know how to live as a gay man not knowing someone who died of AIDS. What has shaped me as a gay man has kept me safe.

While I survived those years with my health intact, I am battered, bruised, and damaged. In 1983, as I was settling into my dorm in my freshman year, *New York* magazine reported there were already 1,096 new AIDS cases in New York City and 864 deaths. And the numbers kept rising; just a year later there were 1,841 new cases and 1,960 deaths.

Grandma and Grandpa now spend their days going to doctors' appointments and friends' funerals. My friends and I did that in our twenties.

In my twenty-second year I went to a funeral or memorial every weekend—for men around my age, friends, but also for strangers. Each time I went to a friend's funeral I knew I moved up in line, closer to when it would be me being eulogized. I attended services for strangers because I wanted to give them their due, to bear witness that they were here. I came to hear stories about them so their stories wouldn't be buried. To this day, I remember anecdotes from the short, vibrant lives of these men. I thought then I wished I knew them: James the actor, who when asked by a doctor "Who is the president?," answered "Colleen Dewhurst," the then president of Actors' Equity Association. My friend Peter, who hooked up in the Tiffany's vault with a salesclerk only to get locked in overnight.

Once a test for HIV was developed, I delayed taking it for fear the government was just rounding up our names to quarantine us. I finally did get tested because I had been sick with a flu for two weeks that would not go away, so my doctor said, "We need to test you for HIV." It was never noted as record in my medical chart; my doctor made a seemingly haphazard mark on my chart that no one else could have deciphered but meant to him that I had been tested. Back then it took two agonizing weeks to get the results.

The grief, the dread, the fear, the carefulness, is my ball and chain. It goes where I go. You are not weighed down by any of this. It's a history lesson for you. You are what I dreamed of being—set free from disease, death, despair. You won't be walking the razor's edge as I did. Your horizon is much farther away than mine was; you can dream big and long-term and not fear not living to see it realized. You can meet a man as an equal, not as an infector; you can kiss and touch and taste without both hands tied behind your back and your mouth closed.

Can you keep as safe as I have without knowing someone who died? Can you be as careful having never visited a friend in the hospital? If you haven't been to a funeral for someone in their twenties; seen parents burying their children; or, worse, watched children buried without parents because they were disowned, how can you have the stamina to be safe? How will you stay safe if you have never promised a friend you'd be with them when they die?

I would ask you to think about what "manageable disease" means. What would it take to manage it? At what cost? How many pills a day? What dosage of drugs would it take? How many doctors' appointments monthly? What's the wear and tear on your body? So take some of my fear and protect yourself. Adopt from my era the requisite condom rule at all times.

The manageable disease I have been dealing with all these years is grief. It's cunning, insidious, and not curable; it never goes away. It flares up at unexpected moments brought on by a long-forgotten scent, the unexpected street you find yourself walking, a taste you vaguely remember. It flattens you when your college roommate dies of AIDS twenty-two years after you first lived together. It roars back when you see twin boys playing together in the playground.

My senior year of college I produced an AIDS benefit called High Spirits. We closed the show with a new song that Michael Callen, my safe-sex guru, had written and gave me permission to use. It is titled "Love Don't Need a Reason," and it ends with the lyric *"Love is all we have, what we don't have is time."* That was my lasting impression—of how little time I had.

Facing a sense of my own mortality at such a young age did not drive me to succeed quickly nor did it fill me with fatalistic calm. Instead, an urgency came over me: I would use whatever precious time I had to discover and know love.

Dive Heart First

THE ADVICE I have always given to you is to be ambitious in your personal life. There are going to be plenty of people in your life who push you to work hours longer than the normal workday, expecting you to overextend yourself, and situations that pressure you to concentrate on your career. Some of that pressure may likely be self-imposed, as you focus on your pursuits and goals. But only you can prioritize your heart, and ensure that you work to nurture it. Your well-cared-for heart will be evident to all, opening you to those who will add promise and purpose to your life. The noblest ambition is to love someone.

Long-lasting and serious relationships are not heteronormative, but they are still not a predetermined destination for us. Nobody is grooming us to be grooms. Committed relationships and marriage are not necessarily the natural progression in the LGBTQ community. Because being gay doesn't conform, it's easy to extend that nonconformity to your social life. Many in our community forgo marriage, for many reasons, in favor of relationships with no expectations, no commitments, no strings attached. But don't be afraid of strings. Their attachments can ground you but they can also be elastic, allowing you the stretch you need in your life. Create a relationship that doesn't constrict your sense of self, but expands it.

Don't be afraid to take a risk with your feelings. A broken heart is still a feeling heart; it is alive. Taking an emotional risk, for better or for worse, allows you to reflect, to learn, to mend and heal if necessary, and to move forward, growing your heart stronger. Don't fold in.

MY RELATIONSHIP WITH Daddy Jordan is my secure home base that lets me try new things and fail. This base is the most important thing to my sustainability, because in Jordan I have a constant power source, and there are no highs too steep, no lows too harrowing, that give me fear or pause. This freedom takes away any desperation to succeed and releases me from being concerned with anyone's approval of me or of my family. This source of bonded strength softens the edges of hard work and difficult careers, because the matter at hand is at home.

When I was in college I read the book *Safe* by Dennis Cooper. I was so struck by one line, which has stayed with me and morphed into my own goal of a relationship: "Even when loved so intently I don't have to think about concepts like love any longer." But as I learned and evolved and met Jordan, I realized that point of view was wrong for me. I think about my love for Jordan every day. I don't just honor and cherish it; I cultivate it and invest in it and rely on it.

Why do we only have mentors for our careers? Find mentors for the type of relationship you want. Grandma and Grandpa have been married for sixty-five years, and we each can learn a lot from how they achieved such a remarkable union. Ask the people in relationships you admire how they make it work. Clock when you are with couples whose every conversation is a competition or the ones who bicker for sport. Discover how people emotionally support each other in a sustained way. Make relationship goals just as you would career goals. I never understand people who say, "*I'm not looking for a relationship; if it happens it happens.*" We get educated for our work lives and take internships at companies we aspire to be a part of, but we don't put in the same effort to being ready to find the person we will spend our lives with and create a family. That we leave up to chance. I wouldn't live in a house without a foundation. I have the relationship I wanted because *I prioritized having it*—just as I prioritized having children.

Coming Out Is Every Day

OUR DOUBLE VISION requires that we have eyes in the back of our head. Part of the exhausting, scary duality of being a gay American is that while being out, being yourself, living your life in pursuit of happiness, you are never fully at liberty to relax. You always have to be on your guard. You had little struggle coming out and you have gay parents, but ironically, your advantages have left you a disadvantage: you have no gay protective reflex.

This will be the first time you don't live at home, your first time without a curfew. This won't be like when you were eleven years old, and we let you walk home alone in New York City for the first time. I can't surreptitiously trail you as I did that day. Now you are an adult gay man, living an adult gay life in the city. You will be in school with students from around the country and the world. You may feel a different atmosphere surrounding you at college and may even be potentially more at risk. I can't let you leave home without a gay guard.

I didn't fully educate you in all the dangers gay

people live with as you were growing up. I didn't share all the difficulties that I encountered or that our community faced—and continues to face. I tried not to dwell on these, because I wanted you to feel secure. When you were little and we'd go as a family to the park or on a subway ride or shopping, and you'd happily call out, "Daddy Jordan, Daddy," part of me was always clocking who heard you, on the lookout for any danger that we could find ourselves pulled into.

I erected my own guard early, but not early enough. I was in the fourth grade, and students had the choice to take band or chorus. I chose chorus and I was the only boy. The next day when my gym teacher heard what I had done, he told all the other boys to jump on the faggot—and they did. That ugly taunt followed me to junior high school, when my classmates found out I was taking dance lessons and labeled me "ballet fag" (I was taking tap). Ever since then I consciously protected myself. I used to imagine that I had an invisible moat around me that no one could get over unless I lowered the drawbridge. As I got older the moat disappeared, but my defenses only grew stronger. During my entire adult gay life, I have never let down my guard, not once. You aren't even aware that I have one, but it has been essential to keep me safe and, more important, to protect my precious family.

As gay dads, we wanted you to feel secure growing up

and to understand that our family was just like those of your friends. Providing you with that sense of security may have left you vulnerable. For example, you never knew that before each of our memorable family vacations, we made sure that the city, state, country, airline, and accommodations were safe for our family. Or that we always carried your birth certificate in case our parenthood was ever challenged at an airport or, worse, at a local hospital. Similarly, you won't be able to hop on a spring break adventure with friends without first considering your safety and assessing the itinerary for a welcoming environment.

A year after our wedding, a man was verbally assaulted and shot to death for being gay, just a few blocks from our home. Pop, who had walked Jordan down the aisle to me, called us to tell us not to hold hands outside. Even legally married we couldn't let up our vigilance. We are legal, not safe.

It was my gay guard that protected you when your therapist gave me the same advice she said she gives parents of straight teens who are dating: Don't let you close your bedroom door and be alone with your boyfriend. I told her it wasn't the same with straight teens and had to explain that two boys can't sit on a park bench and kiss—they could be beaten up, or worse—so the safest place for you was at home.

You are out, but you are not done coming out.

Coming out never ends. It's every day, numerous times a day, and each presents a critical decision, often needed to be made in a split second, as to your safety, and to the consequences, the price, and the gain of that decision. Keeping yourself safe is paramount, and as a gay person you will always need to be aware of where you are and who is around you. There will be many encounters when you'll have to decide whether to reveal yourself. This pause, this instantaneous evaluation, will guard you and over time help guide you as to when to come out and when not to, whom to come out to and whom not to. There is no shame in staying safe.

No matter how many advances our LGBTQ community continues to make, never let your guard down. I don't hold Jordan's hand in public or kiss him goodbye unless the coast is clear enough—for us, holding hands or showing affection in public can be perilous. Be conscious of what you are saying and who can hear you, whether at a movie theatre or a McDonald's. Take note of your surroundings before you hold hands or kiss, whether on the subway or in a taxi—or anywhere. Don't linger looking at a stranger. If in doubt, don't flirt.

Shortly after graduating from college, I was walking arm in arm in the West Village with a date, and a car sped past us, and someone yelled out, calling us fags, and threw a hard object at us, hitting my companion.

A few years later there was a rash of gay bashings in the Village, and we were warned not to walk alone, and eventually the activist group Queer Nation formed a gay civilian patrol group, the Pink Panthers, to protect the community.

At my first job after graduating from college, I thought I could be out at work because gay men were already working there. It was a theatrical general-management firm—the people who run the day-to-day business of Broadway shows. It was the perfect entry-level position for me—until all our shows closed and there was no longer a job.

My boss told me that either they'd have to lay me off or they could send me on the road with the touring company of *Cats*. I didn't have any other job prospects, and no money to fall back on, but I turned him down. I could have just said *I can't leave New York* or *Touring doesn't interest me*. Instead, I shared the true reason: "I just started dating BD and don't want to leave New York." My boss said, "You can't make your whole life about being gay." He was trying to diminish me, telling me to make my gayness smaller till he was comfortable with how gay I was.

Even though I had a lot of trouble finding gainful employment for a long time after that, I didn't regret my decision. The hours I spent babysitting and doing odd jobs were worth it. I made the right decision. BD and I were together for fifteen years, and you are the remarkable gift of that relationship.

MY DEFENSES ARE always up and so are Jordan's. When we flew down to Virginia a couple of years ago to go with Cindy for the twenty-week ultrasound, the hotel receptionist who checked us in asked us what we were doing in town. Both Daddy Jordan and I paused, then he quickly calculated the risk and decided to share with her the fact that we were there to have a baby. The woman was thrilled for us. You'll learn as you get older when to give someone a chance to pleasantly surprise you.

The first non–family member, nonfriend, whom I came out to when I was in college was my doctor. I had a rash and went back to Long Island to see him. I was sure I had AIDS, but before he examined me I knew I had to tell him I was gay. He called my rash—this condition that I was certain was life-threatening—mild crotch rot, merely a result of not drying enough after showering. As for my being gay, he casually, and without much interest or expertise, said, "You're being safe, right?"

My strangest coming-out moment was when we took your brother Boaz to the funeral home moments before we left Modesto with you to the safer environs of San Francisco. By time time my mom had flown in and BD's family drove down, so we all went together to organize Boaz's cremation. Even after we told the funeral director that BD and I were the parents, he didn't understand and kept looking at our sad group, asking who the parents were.

As gay parents, we have had to come out at every playdate, doctor's appointment, music class, and sports program.

Even though you are now out, you'll find that you still need to decide whether and when to come out to your professors, doctors, dentists, landlords, employers, and coworkers. And while coming out is always your own decision, I strongly urge you to tell your college roommates. Don't make your dorm room, your first freedom space away from home, a closet.

In an ideal world, I would want you to be unabashedly out everywhere, all the time, but you can't be. You need to develop your intuition, your sense of safety and of danger, to know when the time is right and when it is not. I certainly have resolved to being out to the world, especially when I knew I was in environments where I was the only gay person, or one of very few—like in temple, or shopping for diapers, or at your school's Back-to-School nights—but I always sized up my harm quotient and assessed the risk before acting. Remember: Your first responsibility is to your safety.

There will be times when no one will know you are gay. And you may think that not everyone needs to know you are gay—I, personally, don't believe that. If most of the time the majority of people think I am straight, I want to disabuse them of that notion. But passing because you can is why you have a choice: it's tantamount to hiding in plain sight. My choice has always been *not* to hide when I was safe enough not to. Not all in our community can do that. The bravest among us cannot pass. All the perceived reasons that someone is gay or different that have so many of us living in crushing fear every day makes my passing unacceptable. Staying silent too has consequences—to your heart, to your mental and emotional stability, to your gay self-esteem. Balance your safety with your sturdy heart. You may find that you are in the minority in many, if not most, of the situations you are in, so speaking up, speaking out, will always have to be a conscious decision. It is not enough to let people assume what they want, because usually they will assume you're straight—and voilà, you've magically passed. But passing is not emotionally sustainable.

Being safe enough to be out is a privilege and a responsibility. You won't always know the benefit it would be to someone to come in contact with a gay person, a tiny ripple of gay. When Jordan and I were first courting, we were at dinner at an upscale restaurant, and we were sitting across from each other, talking, and we were holding hands atop the table. A woman came up to us and asked if we were gay, and we said yes. She said, "Could I ask you a question?" She sat down at our table and started to cry. She was from Texas and she was visiting New York City with friends. She told us that her husband had just come out to her, and she wanted to know if we had always known we were gay, and if we thought her husband had known this whole time and if her marriage had been a lie. She didn't know any gay people. We explained to her that each person's journey to understand himself is unique, that there is no set timetable. We were still holding hands as we talked, and she put her hands over ours. We all held hands as Jordan and I told this stranger that we truly believed her husband loved her when they got married, and that he still does.

PRIDE ISN'T JUST for a parade one day a year. It is not a miniature rainbow flag or rubber bracelet with a corporate logo on it given freely on that day, like beads tossed during Mardi Gras. Pride is foremost our gay self-esteem, but it is also our bond with everyone in the LGBTQ community, everywhere. Pride is our unique way of letting everyone know that we are here, that we belong in this world. If we can say we are gay, we must not do so just to make our own lives better, easier, more transparent, and authentic. We do so to clear a path for those who can't come out—for all the people who live in places where their freedom is not a given or who don't feel safe in their own families—to make inroads in the straight world for them. Each time we come out, we send up a flare of hope and direction, showing the way.

Words Matter

BEING OUT MATTERS. What you do being out matters. Not accepting anyone putting you in a box or pushing you to the sidelines matters. The members of our community have to protect against the insidious ways we are kept down and out.

Daddy Jordan and I have always taught you that words matter, and we told you "you can hurt your own feelings" with the words you use to describe yourself. We told you not to undercut yourself with harmful language. A new, seemingly positive, celebratory word has joined the lexicon. Now that actors, politicians, athletes, and CEOs have publicly declared themselves gay, the media refer to them as "openly gay"—we even refer to ourselves that way.

The media reports as if they still consider being called gay a slur, so they use *openly* to point out they didn't use the epithet first. *Openly* is a noxious term that is not as accepting or as enlightened as it seems. It expresses surprise, shock, that someone gay is actually, officially, not hiding in plain sight. *Openly* applauds audaciousness, signaling that an out gay person is not the norm and that this particular gay person isn't as shameful as warranted.

Openly gay reinforces the negative; it substantiates a disapproving origin. There is more power in the simple, unqualified statement: I am gay.

You may wonder why someone who is gay needs to mention it at all. Gay isn't merit; it just is. Visibility saves lives, and our concealment erases us—a slow death by imperceptibility. Akin to career day in elementary school, every time we note a gay firefighter, a gay doctor, a gay police officer, a gay teacher, a gay pop star, a gay presidential candidate, we provide possibility—and very often a lifeline, or a light through a dark tunnel. Because it saves young LGBTQ lives to see gay people who are integrated into every part of our culture.

IS BEING GAY a choice, or were you born this way? I never engage in this conversation, and I have been asked this a lot, as you will be.

Our political organizations dissuade us from having this debate because anti-gay activists harp on gay as merely a sexual preference, a choice, which would mean being gay can be cured. In the Supreme Court, our being gay as an "immutable" trait is critical because it affords us the heightened scrutiny our equal protection relies on. We require the judgment that our gayness is a trait that would be abhorrent for society to expect us to disavow. Born this way leads to the law of equality.

That is all vitally important, but I don't argue in court, so I reject the premise of the question. It comes from straight parents needing us to be born gay so they can be absolved of blame. We are asked by straight friends trying to make sense of us. What is the answer they are after? What is the intent of the question? Is it to reinforce their superiority? Comfort their teenage questioning and experimentation? Or is it meant to diminish us and marginalize us? Are they sympathizing with our helplessness over nature or, worse, nurture? Is their preferred answer *I was born this way, I can't help it; I am stricken, stuck*—?

If I were to answer *I was born this way, I didn't choose it*, the logical conclusion is that *I would not choose it*—that of course I would choose to be straight, that of course I really wish I were straight. That is not an acceptable outcome. I will not give anyone the impression that being a gay person, living a gay life, is not enviable. If it is a choice, I'd choose it.

It's Still a Straight Man's World

A T A FAMILY dinner a few years ago, we found ourselves alienated when a relative declared that
a baker should not be forced to bake a cake for a gay
wedding. During this casual conversation, the relative
seemed to be speaking about a civil rights issue as non-
chalantly as if he were discussing people's preferences
for chocolate over vanilla, but to me it felt as though
he was diminishing our personhood. A member of our
own family was attempting to explain to us that it
was logical that who we are doesn't mean that we are
entitled to all the rights that everyone else around that
table has.

When Trump became president, the disconnect
that exists within our family was laid bare as never before. Some in our family voted for Trump and backed
him even after we warned that he and Mike Pence
were a dangerous threat to us, and they continue to
support him even now. I see it as a painful betrayal.
After they pulled the lever for him and were proud
guests at his inauguration, you rightfully asked how

they could support someone who wants our family to disappear.

The only way I can make sense of the fact that the allyship of some in our family hasn't extended to where we want it to be is that they do not fully appreciate how important being gay is to who we are and to all of who we are. They do not understand all the parts of our lives that require vigilance and that demand our singular focus. Our double vision is necessary even at our own Thanksgiving table.

I should have been ready. When I saw the White House blazing with rainbow lights that incredible June evening in 2015, celebrating the Supreme Court's ruling on Marriage Equality, I should have known. But the majesty was intoxicating, the great decades-in-waiting sigh of relief was overwhelming. I should have known a backlash would be coming for us; I should have been ready for this fierce straight-lash after eight years of a black president, a woman running to succeed him, Marriage Equality the law of the land, transgender service members being allowed to serve in the military, the repeal of Don't Ask, Don't Tell. How naive of me, after everything I had experienced and with all that I know, to let myself believe that the colorful lighting display illuminating our nation's first house was our real country.

The morning after Trump was elected, Harvey called me and said, "The only positive is that now we know where we are. We thought we were one place and that our country was one thing, and now we know where we really are."

And the most hurtful irony of all is that you are now susceptible to the straight-lash against the increased acceptance and visibility of gay people that I have fought for my entire adult life.

Alarmingly, surveys show that 60 percent of lesbian, gay, and bisexual Americans and 78 percent of transgender Americans have experienced discrimination. Just as you leave our home, the Gay and Lesbian Alliance Against Defamation's (GLAAD) 2018 survey shows straight Americans' comfort level decreased in three measured areas—with a gay family member, with a gay doctor, and with a child having a gay teacher. The same survey in 2019 showed a further decline among eighteen- to thirty-four-year-olds. The Southern Poverty Law Center reports that there are forty-five anti-LGBTQ organizations spread over twenty-one states. Currently there are more than one hundred anti-LGBTQ bills in state legislatures, thirty states in all—local control bills (which prevent cities or local governments from passing nondiscrimination protections greater than their state offers), anti-trans bills, anti-marriage legislation, and the absurdly titled religious freedom bills. These bills are designed to be challenged, to weave their way up to the Supreme Court, and if these bills are upheld, would embolden other states.

Hate crimes against LGBTQ people are on the rise, with alarming statistics: at least twenty-six transgender people were killed in 2018, and as of October 2019, there have already been eighteen more murders. Now Trump and Pence have an aggressive and widespread effort to enact anti-LGBTQ policies across the government. They are literally erasing gay people by instructing agencies not to collect data on us. President Obama had taken the position that sex discrimination included sexual orientation and gender identity; Trump has reversed that. There are currently three vital cases before the Supreme Court in which the court will decide which of them is correct. The Department of Education has stopped investigating transgender student complaints about access to bathrooms. There is no enforcement at the US departments of Health and Human Services (HHS), Housing and Urban Development (HUD), and Education for sexual orientation discrimination. The HHS has created a conscience and religious freedom division to offer greater protections for health-care workers who do not wish to treat LGBTQ patients, and it has finalized and set its conscience rule (currently subject to litigation), which permits health-care personnel not to participate in a patient's care in which the provider has religious or moral objections. In this government, the Hippocratic Oath clearly has its limits. The Department of Justice (DOJ) has started a religious task force to expand the scope of denying services or refusing to hire LGBTQ people. The wall America really needs is not on the southern border; it's between church and state.

Our brief liberation has emboldened our adversaries. They saw a house that they believe belongs only to them lit in our rainbow colors, and in a lot of ways now it is going to be even harder for you than it was for me. When I was eighteen, so much of what we have now seemed like a pipe dream to us—and a nightmare for those against us—but with so much realized, what seemed hard to imagine for all of us actually came to pass. So now the Family Research Council and Focus on the Family won't stop until all our newly minted rights, our visibility, our respectability, our representation, and our allyship are dismantled. Anti-LGBTQ bills are nothing more than a systematic weaponizing of American religious bigotry designed to strip you of your Constitutional guarantees.

Trump has reinstated the ban on transgender Americans serving in the military; HUD intends to issue a new rule allowing shelters receiving federal funding to ban access to transgender homeless people; the HHS has issued a proposal for a new rule withdrawing gender-identity protections from the Affordable Care Act; and the DOJ argued in support of a baker who denied services to a gay couple during the Supreme Court's oral arguments for the case *Masterpiece Cakeshop v. Colorado Civil Rights Commission*. Marriage

Equality will be like *Roe v. Wade*, a political rallying cry for evangelicals and a craven Republican Party, picked at by courts and chipped away at by state legislatures, at risk of being eradicated. Long after Trump is gone, his voters and judges will remain.

How heartbreaking that your entrée into Gay America doesn't feel so different from mine after all. The only difference is that I grew up in an America virtually devoid of gay visibility and gay rights, and you have seen and experienced gay life since birth, and now you are coming out into an America trying to undo it all and erase us. When you first told us that you were gay, I was relieved that so much had changed, that you were at least becoming an adult during the upward swing to greater freedoms and equality. Now all that has changed, and you and your peers are at risk just as previous generations were. I always knew I was a gay man in a straight man's world. Remember that you are too now.

Just having the debate over these discriminatory bills endangers lives, a continuation of our nation's shameful abuse of our LGBTQ youth. Conversion therapy remains legal to perform on minors in thirty-two states. Our kids are listening, and whether these horrid bills become law or not, the damage has begun, and our brothers and sisters are going to either stay firmly in their closets or, I fear, do harm to themselves. The Trevor Project, which provides crisis-intervention and suicide-prevention services to LGBTQ young people under twenty-five, had double the call volume the day after Trump was elected, and calls spike every time there are anti-LGBTQ policies and rhetoric coming from the administration. Call volume continues to climb and is at the highest level in the hotline's twenty-one-year history. We must make our world kinder and safer for our kids to come out into and join in.

There is currently no federal law that bans LGBTQ discrimination. There is now a new bill pending in Congress that would ban discrimination in employment, housing, credit, public accommodations, education, federal financial assistance, and federal jury service. The Equality Act would amend existing law, including the Civil Rights Act of 1964, the Fair Housing Act, the Equal Credit Opportunity Act, and the Jury Selection and Service Act. And to shore up the vital separation of church and state, the Religious Freedom Restoration Act could not be used as a defense for discrimination on any basis.

In addition to Pride parades, it is time for an LGBTQ March on Washington to reject the tide of hate and violence, to protect our LGBTQ youth, and to demand passage of the Equality Act.

How will your diverse, fluid, lulled young gay community galvanize? It is time to circle the wagons. All those in our now porous community will have to rise up for one another. Do not think that each of your disparate group's struggles aren't your battle to fight. LGBTQ is our seal, just as the original American motto declares: *E Pluribus Unum*—"Out of Many, One."

WHEN YOU WERE five years old, we were so proud that you could identify so many states on the map of the USA that hung in your room. Now you need to learn Gay Geography—you need to know all the states and their anti-LGBTQ laws. Every state has different laws, and you must be aware of them before you visit or think about moving and living elsewhere.

Where you go to college, where you visit for spring break, where you look for internships and jobs, where you start your family, now involves a serious game of hopscotch. The Human Rights Campaign's State Equality Index is the GPS you need for traversing this country. Their Municipal Equality Index evaluates cities on inclusive municipal laws, policies, and services for LGBTQ people. Your America isn't all the fifty states you memorized as a child—it's not Oklahoma, where you can be denied being an adoptive parent; not North Carolina, Tennessee, or Kansas, states that call our marriages parodies by ignoring the Supreme Court and working to enact laws that define marriage as a union between a man and a woman. Twenty-eight states do not have laws that prohibit discrimination on the basis of sexual orientation—56 percent of the country. That severely narrows your employment opportunities.

Foreign travel is perilous as well, so studying abroad, traveling, or working all now have to include the determining factor of your safety. The big, wide world we taught you to be curious about and told you was full of wonder now constricts you, your path diminishing.

AFTER THE MASSACRE at the Pulse nightclub, the Orlando gay bar where forty-nine people were killed, I took you to Stonewall. You and I stood at the vigil in front of the bar where the flames of the gay civil rights movement were ignited, a memorial of flowers on the ground, a sign in the window reading STOP THE HATE. It felt so familiar to me, a crime of hate and deadly violence toward gays once again resigning me to Stonewall, now being pulled from the light back into darkness. Stonewall doesn't have that force for you.

Stonewall is now, amazingly, a National Monument, just as significant as the Statue of Liberty and the African Burial Ground. But it isn't a dusty historic relic; it's not just a soothing gay touchstone. It is the physical manifestation of our journey, of our progress. It's our movement's mood ring. It shines bright violet when we celebrate, turns ashen in our collective sadness, and burns red as a repository for our rage. Its history doesn't render it obsolete; its existence is a promise, an energy source. My yo-yo relationship with Stonewall is maddening, variably lifting to elation then rolling down to despair. But we remain committed to each other.

That day was the first time I took you to Stonewall. We went to mourn. As I watched you read the notes left with the flowers, I thought of all the other times I had been there. I called Harvey from there in 1986, when I was celebrating the New York City Council's passage of a gay rights bill, banning discrimination on the basis of sexual orientation in housing, employment, and public accommodations, and from the pay phone relayed the euphoric scene for him. I returned three months later in dizzying speed to protest the Supreme Court's *Hardwick v. Bowers* ruling, which was described by Tom Stoddard of Lambda Legal Defense and Education Fund as "our Dred Scott case." In Justice Byron White's majority opinion, he compared homosexuality with adultery, incest, and sex crimes. Chief Justice Warren Burger had written in his concurring opinion: "To hold that the act of homosexual sodomy is somehow protected as a fundamental right would be to cast aside millennia of moral teaching." That disastrous decision was made as AIDS deaths were mounting, it was combustible, and we were in a fury. Soon after, ACT UP unleashed our power.

I remembered being at Stonewall with Jordan in June 2011, crying with happiness when the New York State Legislature passed the Marriage Equality Act. I was drawn again to Stonewall in 2013, to celebrate

Edie Windsor and the fall of the disastrous Defense of Marriage Act (DOMA); ran excitedly there to join the euphoria in 2015 over the *Obergefell* decision; and was forced back in 2017 for a LGBTQ solidarity rally when Trump was elected. Our upward rise has always been followed by a countering, the maddening pendulum between the celebration and the fight, within our double vision.

We stood there that day mourning the Pulse victims and I cried. I cried for the lives taken, for the injured, and for the parents' unspeakable losses. At that moment I was sad to be back there at Stonewall, and angry that now, through catastrophe, you are connected to this small bar on Christopher Street. That could have been you among those murdered at Pulse that night, or wherever the next gay massacre may be—and in my heart I know there will be another. You will go to gay bars with friends, dance at gay clubs, be on a street with a boyfriend or a date, and you will be a target. I cried tears of worry for you.

STONEWALL DOESN'T COURSE through your veins as it does mine. Standing where decades of LGBTQ people before you have stood, being on the street where so many lives were lived and lost, meeting on the same sidewalk where Marsha P. Johnson and Sylvia Rivera fought back—this will embolden you. It will illustrate for you the long line of people you are now among, who have held ground in the same spot, demanding that their humanity be recognized and protected. You will, in front of the red neon lights, step into the timeline with rightful, rageful indignation. Standing on Christopher Street outside a small beating-heart bar, you will understand where you come from.

Being a Good Gay Citizen

I AM OLD ENOUGH to remember when we were "Gay"; now we are "LGBTQ." Our combined identities are not just stripes on our flag so everyone feels represented; our initialism is our chain linking us together— we rise and fall, survive and thrive, only if we all do. Those who want to do us harm aren't parsing out our letters to simply pick off just one of us. They strike first at the most vulnerable and continue down the line.

You are leaving home and entering a riptide of hate, and we taught you as a child never to swim directly into a riptide, always swim with it, parallel to where you want to be. Not so with this fierce current. Here you have to join the battle to fight just as I did. The only way to safe shore is forward. It is our collective responsibility to fight every injustice and to defeat every bad bill everywhere. This demands all our participation. Being gay is, still, acting up and fighting back.

Your civic duty now includes your volunteering for organizations like the Human Rights Campaign, the largest national LGBTQ civil rights organization; or Lambda Legal Defense, the national legal organization committed to achieving full recognition of the civil rights of LGBTQ people and everyone living with HIV; or The Trevor Project; or grassroots organizations like ACT UP, still united in anger and committed to direct action to end the AIDS crisis; or new groups you can seek out.

Being a good gay citizen requires voting. As important as allies are, they aren't LGBTQ-centric voters as you must be at every election for every office, from the Board of Education officials up to the president of the United States. Do not let anyone dismiss your activism as identity politics. That charge usually comes from straight people treating us like a distraction.

Identity politics doesn't narrow your focus; it widens your expectations of candidates and forces them to directly address our community and our issues. It claims your rightful attention.

Identity politics doesn't silo you. The power of identity politics is to find what other identities you identify with. Look for the winning coalition that will bring liberty and justice for all. If we are to restore and expand our rights, then we also have to recognize that we are not unique in being under attack. Women, people of color, immigrants, the poor, also have the same stake as we do in who the next president will be. To be sure, we have common oppressors and mutual goals. We all need to ensure our individual communities are being heard, while also listening and standing up for one another. Then eventually we must coalesce around the winning vision that includes all of us.

The 2020 Democratic presidential primary is thrilling due to the diversity of its candidates, including the extraordinary Pete Buttigieg, the mayor of South Bend, Indiana, and a gay man. There is no way to be cavalier about a gay man being a top-tier contender for the presidency. It is remarkable. And when someone tries to use Mayor Pete as proof there is no more homophobia, just point out where racism stands after we had our first black president for eight years.

Beware too the Republican allies who tell you they are fiscally conservative but socially liberal. They are telling you that our community will always come second to them. Their wallet, their tax rate, dwarfs our right to exist. An alleged LGBTQ ally who votes for a Republican presidential candidate knowing full well that contender will appoint conservative judges, especially to the Supreme Court, is not allied with us.

Who is elected at every level has consequences. An elected county clerk in Kentucky defied a federal court order to issue marriage licenses to same-sex couples because of her own personal religious beliefs.

Vote as if your life depends on it, because it does. Vote as if someone else's life depends on it too, because it does. Ask which candidate will aggressively and progressively improve the lives of LGBTQ people. Think about all the Supreme Court cases that have had profound and real effect on our lives—*Bowers v. Hardwick* rendered us noncitizens, and seventeen years later *Lawrence v. Texas* overturned *Bowers*, finding that lesbians and gay men have the same fundamental right to private sexual intimacy with another adult as heterosexuals do, and the marriage cases: *United States v. Windsor* in 2013 and *Obergefell v. Hodges* in 2015.

Being a good gay citizen means being informed. I remember when the only place I was able to get my gay news was from *The Native.* Now articles about us appear in mainstream media with some regularity, but not everything that matters to us makes it in, so stay informed, and by LGBTQ journalists and LGBTQ news outlets. I've bought you subscriptions to *The Advocate* and *Out* magazine. Read websites like New-NowNext, the HuffPost's Queer Voices, them., and Queerty; blogs like Towleroad and JoeMyGod. Follow LGBTQ journalists and thinkers on Twitter, like Zach Stafford, Jennifer Finney Boylan, Tim Teeman, Scott Bixby, Saeed Jones, Chase Strangio, Zack Ford, Sarah Schulman, David Artavia, Andrew Sullivan, Jonathan Capehart, Rachel Maddow, Tre'vell Anderson, Phillip Picardi, and Janet Mock. Look for the regional LGBTQ periodicals and websites wherever you live.

LGBTQ people span every race, religion, and culture. We are women, people of color, people with disabilities, immigrants, refugees. Don't get caught in the senseless competition between marginalized groups as to who is more oppressed. The Oppression Olympics serve one group and one purpose—the oppressors, and to divide and conquer.

Remember what your Gay-Straight Alliance adviser pointed out when he told you that your committed student group wasn't just for the kids inside the room, but was especially for the kids not yet ready or able to walk in the door. He said they were comforted just knowing your group existed. Keep going to Pride for the people who can't. For those LGBTQ people not yet out, oppressed, who live in fear for their lives or livelihoods, who live in countries that would condemn and kill them—go to Pride for them. Show them by our vast numbers that what awaits them is a sea of acceptance and love.

I WAS BLESSED to have Harvey be the gentle (and sometimes not so gentle) guide for my gay life. AIDS robbed us of a lifetime of mentors, a devastating tragedy for our younger generations that missed out on their wisdom, knowledge, experiences, and fabulousness. That is one void we all can fill. The Point Foundation provides mentorship and scholarship funding for LGBTQ students of merit. You aren't too young to start helping someone else. Don't wait till you are in the middle of your life or at the end of it to start to help. There is no such thing as giving back, no such thing as paying it forward. Part of living, part of the doing, is helping other people. It's not a debt; it's the purpose. You can't consider yourself successful if you aren't helping someone else to get where you are. And you are never too young to start.

It has been the work of my adult life to understand deeply that the best part of me is reviled, my proudest aspect assaulted. I've had to ward off and fight back violence, disease, hate, and condemnation. I've worked to amplify my own being, not just for the right to exist, to be left alone, but to thrive and to shine. The pursuit of happiness isn't just a declaration; it's a dare to live. It's not just about law; it's about my potential. It's not only about access; it's about ascending. To live as fully gay as possible is how I am most alive.

Every gay person is a wonder. It takes enormous effort to go from cocoon to butterfly and to stay aloft daily, to defy your parents' expectations, your religious teachers, to get through childhood knowing you are different, and to stand up and say this is me when everything around you tells you to be something else, to withstand the daily reminders that make you feel isolated.

The reason the straight world tries to diminish us, to demean our differences, is not because we are defective or worthless. Quite the contrary: it is because they know how powerful being gay makes us.

We don't learn about ourselves in history class, don't learn sex-ed; we are bullied and bruised by classmates.

We sit in Sunday schools that tell us we're sinful. We are minorities within our own families, disappointments to our parents and to our ancestral status quo. We are subjected to the shifting wins and whims of a biased American electorate and a jaundiced judiciary.

Each of us is keenly aware that our perception of ourselves stands in stark contrast to the field of vision of our country. Most of this abuse takes place while we are children. What is in our hearts, what is most special about us, we are told is wrong and to suppress it. How remarkable it is that, among all these terrors, we still come out. We still rise and say this is me. Our power to resist, persist, act up, fight back, is in fact the spirit of an extraordinary species of people.

I have invested my time in unlocking what gay had in store for me. I believed since I was a child that for some reason I was chosen, and discovering what that meant, unraveling its glory, understanding its mystery, and respecting its power is why I get to say I am your father. I didn't hide, ignore, or scrub off my gayness at any part of my life. The theme of my life has been to fulfill all the parts of my gay self and to imbue the world with more gay.

You don't have to be gay like me, but you do need to be sufficiently gay your own way. I didn't do everything right—and I have the scars to show for it. But you have been chosen too, and it's not an accident; it's your power. What is different now isn't all better, and what's worse is just as scary, so our lives will look very different and painfully similar.

Keep focused your two visions—in one, the struggle and complications; and in the other, all your worthy, glorious gayness. At four years old you were prescribed glasses—a health remnant of your prematurity. I chose glasses for you that you hated, and Daddy Jordan took you to find ones that you liked and would actually wear. You settled on a particular brand, and when the salesclerk showed you the sample with all the color options, you said you wanted that exact pair. You chose rainbow glasses and have ever since worn the same multicolor, vibrant frames. You have literally looked out of rainbow glasses your whole life. Your glasses have always helped you to see the world better.

Stonewall50

THE RAINBOWS STARTED creeping out just after Memorial Day, like Christmas trees on every corner the Friday after Thanksgiving. Nobody could escape that June was Pride Month. Oh, yes—Pride is now a full month. That in and of itself is astonishing. And this year was the fiftieth anniversary of the Stonewall Uprising, so WorldPride converged on New York City with shock and awe. It also coincided with the last Pride before you leave home for college, so I had a lot of emotions.

I had spent the month trying not to miss any of the Stonewall commemorative reads in newspapers, magazines, and online. There were countless lectures, shows, and concerts all over New York City. I watched documentaries on the Stonewall uprisings on PBS and Here TV. I visited the New York Public Library and the New-York Historical Society to see their Stonewall50 exhibits, and as I wandered their hallowed halls, peering at photographs of protests, arrests, violence, and harassment, it all felt as though it was being presented as ancient history. *Look what gays used to go through!*

The rainbows used to feel like a big hug to me, but now they seem more like an exclamation point proclaiming that the struggle is over. *Congratulations, you've reached the Promised Land!* All month the rainbows were trying to force me to be happy. These trails of colors were to lead us all together to celebrate. But this June, the fiftieth anniversary of Stonewall, wasn't a time to celebrate; it was a time to fight back and to stem all that imperils us. I didn't want to collude with all these colors—not now. There is an epidemic of transgender people being murdered; why are we all not donning targets and organizing in mass protest? Each time I passed another creative use of a rainbow—painted on the crosswalk, baked into the gooey inside of a cookie, adorned on T-shirts, and socks, and subway cars—I felt bullied by corporations and tourist boards into compliant submission. *You should be happy for all that you have.*

The rainbow is colorful, playful, joyful, and childlike. Imagine how many of these global corporations and brands would be in our march, would market to us, would stand with us, if the pink triangle were our symbol instead. Would pink triangles be put up all over cities signifying June as Pride Month? Would water bottles be sold with the more startling, historically loaded symbol? Would they be slapped on store windows?

Like you, I was never taught the story of the pink

triangle during my study of the Holocaust in either my high school or Hebrew school. The pink triangle, the symbol the Nazis forced homosexuals in the concentration camps to wear, was decades later reclaimed by gay activists as a symbol of positive gay self-identity, and to me that triangle always felt urgent, dangerous, rebellious. The first item I ever purchased at the Oscar Wilde Memorial Bookshop was an enamel pink triangle pin, and I affixed it to my jean jacket and wore it all through college.

FROM THE FIRST of the month it was impossible to walk anywhere in Manhattan, and many other parts of New York City, without seeing the words *Pride* and *Love Is Love*. I found them cloying. They obscure the war that has been declared on us, the violence that we face daily.

When the big Pride weekend was upon us, I checked in with a friend to find out what his Pride plans were. He texted me his busy itinerary of events: On Friday he was attending a black-tie fund-raiser at the tony (and ironically named) Rainbow Room, then later that night he'd head to a disco in Brooklyn. On Saturday night he was hosting a cocktail party at his apartment before going dancing, and then on Sunday—the actual Gay Pride Day—he was off to brunch, then a party at Soho House, and in the evening he'd go to Pier 97 to catch Madonna's concert to close out WorldPride. I asked him what about the Queer Liberation March or the Pride parade? He said he would stop by the parade. Later he told me that he didn't end up stopping by after all; he just happened to only pass by as he traveled from one social event to another.

On the actual fiftieth anniversary of the Stonewall Uprising—Friday, June 28, 2019—I went with Jordan to hear him give a short speech inside Stonewall at the Pride Live Stonewall Day Concert. Lady Gaga was scheduled to appear, and Christopher Street was packed with people and cordoned off by cops. When we walked into the bar—this small, old, sacred space—we were overcome with emotion. My mind flashed back to all the extraordinary Fred W. McDarrah black-and-white photos of those fateful nights fifty years ago and of the early marches he captured and that I had just viewed at the Stonewall50 exhibits. I looked at the faces of all the different people huddled together in the bar now celebrating. We didn't look all that different from the people who stood in this same spot in 1969.

On Saturday I drove to New Jersey to address Affirmation: LGBTQ Mormons, Families & Friends. As my GPS wove me around the streets of Ridgewood, I noticed one lone rainbow flag with the word *Hope* stitched on it, hung outside a home in this American suburb. This one solo rainbow flag had a different effect on me. It was isolated and stoic, proud. Seeing a single rainbow flag fly is a very different experience than seeing your city awash in them. I caught myself: I realized it was a privilege to complain about their overuse and commercialization.

On Sunday you had your own Pride plans: to go to a rooftop party and watch the parade later in the afternoon. I put on my @TheAIDSMemorial T-shirt (whose logo is a pink triangle), Jordan helped Levi put on his noise-canceling headphones, and we went to line up for the Queer Liberation March. We wanted Levi to start the practice and habit of showing up. The Queer Liberation March assembled outside Stonewall and traced the same route that the original 1970 Gay Liberation March took. This alternative—no corporations, no floats, less police presence, fewer barricades—was organized by the Reclaim Pride Coalition, activists decrying the commercialization of the main parade and trying to make it a protest again.

We started the march with ACT UP, at Sheridan Square, then northward on Seventh Avenue to West Tenth Street, where I passed my first New York City apartment. It was the apartment that I shared with Ron, who later died of AIDS. I walked up the stoop so I could tell my twenty-one-year-old self, *Yes, can you fucking believe it? We still have to march, still have to fight all these years later for our right to exist peacefully*, and to tell Ron that I miss him and that I think about him often.

The fire station next door had set up a folding table

like a kid's lemonade stand, and the firefighters were selling FDNY Pride T-shirts.

The Queer Liberation March was much like I remembered my first Pride Marches, when you could walk in and out without restriction, unlike the main event now, which is very restricted. We marched among hand-painted signs and joined in the angry chants. There was a moment of silence, and ACT UP staged two "die-ins," a demonstration the group became notorious for in the 1980s and '90s when AIDS was ravaging the community. An astounding forty-five thousand people showed up to participate, and we saw more fists than flag waving. Jordan, Levi, and I moved ahead and marched with Voices4, an activist group fighting for global LGBTQ liberation. This group was full of young demonstrators all dressed in the same white T-shirt with pink triangle and pink eye makeup to match. They each held signs that had messages from LGBTQ people from around the world who couldn't march, who couldn't be out. These activists were the voices for these people, carrying and delivering their messages:

I STRUGGLE TO LOVE WHO I AM BECAUSE MY COUNTRY NEVER WILL. EGYPT.

I AM FROM INDONESIA AND NO WE CAN'T CELEBRATE PRIDE HERE OPENLY LIKE A PARADE. I'M 24 BISEXUAL MUSLIM.

Jordan took a picture of one poster with the message WE DESERVE TO EXIST, TOO. (KUWAIT). He posted that picture on Instagram with the caption "Messages from those who cannot march."

IN THE AFTERNOON, Jordan stayed home while your brother napped (our Pride plans now expanded to include Levi's nap schedule), and I went to the parade. I waited at police barricade after police barricade so I could get to Fifth Avenue to view the parade. It took an hour for me to make it to where I could see my first float just ten blocks from our apartment. Very different from that morning.

On my way to commemorate that fateful night and honor the people who fought back police harassment and abuse, I passed by a police SUV with a big rainbow stripe painted on it, with decals reading EQUITY AND INCLUSION; CELEBRATING DIVERSITY; #SAFEPLACE.

Finally, at Fifth Avenue I saw the magnificent floats sailing magically and, yes, proudly down a sea of rainbows. The parade lasted twelve and a half hours from start to finish, but that's not bloat; it's breadth. I do love this parade—our creativity at full tilt, its honky-tonk vibe, its breathtaking exuberance.

Then there they were—the companies represented with employees full of pride, adorned with matching merchandise. I couldn't help but be moved to see so many recognizable American brands celebrating Pride, their LGBTQ employees, us. It wasn't so long ago that we craved corporate support. Then I remembered that

Judd Legum had just reported in his newsletter "Popular Information" how many of those same companies contribute millions of dollars to anti-LGBTQ elected officials who actively work against us. They use rainbows to cloak their bad behavior. Our need for acceptance so strong that we will take the pink washing and say thanks for the bath. I guess it is a sign of our progress that companies want to appear to be our allies even when they aren't. So I soured on these branded floats that were no more than team-building exercises, more corporate pride than Gay Pride. If all these companies' participation come out of their marketing budgets, they were getting a good bang for their buck, as 2.5 million people showed up. But if the money for Pride was out of their community budgets, we all can think of better uses to support the LGBTQ community. I wondered how many of these companies had members of our community in their positions of leadership. That would be a sign of a real corporate creed.

ALL DAY I stewed in the politics of it all, but then the dancing on the floats, the comrades walking in a contingent, the fervent spectators—what was breathlessly washing over me was that everyone was getting to be themselves and allowing others to be themselves, however they chose. That on this special day, at this appointed time, was the opportunity to rise, rise, rise.

And as for that friend who never made it to the

parade—well, that makes sense too. He had suffered demoralizing discrimination in his former workplace and now devotes his Pride to friendships and feeling free.

As I walked back home to our family, Jordan texted me that he had received a response on the picture of the sign he had posted from Kuwait: THAT'S ME!!! I SENT THAT!!! thank you thank you thank you this means the world to me i'm literally crying thank you.

I realized that the two marches coexisting are right. Our day is as complicated as we are. The two events tell a more complete story of who we are; our narrative has its rage and its release. It is, indeed, Queer.

Nobody has a claim on Pride, and in the end that is the point—to claim your own pride on your own terms. So the tension actually works. It's not a competition, and there's no right or wrong way to do it. It's one, both, or your own way. It's fist and flag; swagger and swag; sex and sentimentality; activists, elders, and kids. It's small nonprofits and corporate powerhouses; it's show and tell; it's rage and rejoicing, pink triangles and rainbows, loss and longing. It's love *as* love.

This Parent's Prayer

I PRAY YOUR LIFE is full of love. I hope it includes activism. I expect you'll be of service.

I hope too through your buoyant colors you wear daily that your life will have a vibrancy, especially now while you are young, that mine did not.

I hope you'll try, and if you fail, try some more.

I wish you to be loved the way I am.

I want you to know the glory is in the doing, not in any reward, financial gain, or accolade.

I want you to aim high, because if you aim for the middle you will find it.

Take time to think: there are no no-brainers.

Crave responsibility; it is where the living is.

Always want the ball.

Be kind. Being kind is like warming up your voice before singing or stretching before an athletic activity. Being kind opens you up to be ready for anything, and being kind to people makes them feel valued. When you are ready for anything, and valuing the people around you, the possibilities of what you can achieve are endless.

Don't look down on anyone unless it's to help pick them up.

Strive to be curious, not just capable.

There is not a finite amount of success in the world. Be the student most likely to want everyone to succeed.

In our loaded-for-bear world, where seemingly everyone has become a disciplinarian, teach don't lecture, guide don't demean, bolster don't belittle.

Honor your parents by being yourself and all of yourself, living fully and unapologetically.

Comfort when needed and cause discomfort when required.

Care for and about yourself. Care for your friends and your family. Care for our community.

YOU ARE LEAVING home to join the greatest of odysseys, taking off on a magical and mysterious adventure. You are on the precipice where so many men before you stood. Jump. Jump as high and as far and as wide as you can.

Daddy Jordan and I are here watching you with utter wonder.

Acknowledgments

MY ETERNAL GRATITUDE to my rare and extraordinary friend Arianna Huffington, who wields her generosity like a magic wand.

Thank you to Lea Carpenter, the first person after my husband whom I told my idea for this book to, whose instantaneous enthusiasm propelled me and whose support sustained me. Thank you to Maureen O'Brien for early and important guidance.

Thank you to my masterful and magnetic agent, Jennifer Rudolph Walsh at WME, who shepherded my book and me with exceptional expertise and care.

I am forever indebted to my brilliant editor and publisher, Jonathan Burnham, whose great insight, intellect, and heart enhanced my book as well as my experience of writing it immeasurably.

There are many organizations that are fighting tirelessly for our LGBTQ community, and I called on several of them during the writing of this book. Thank you so much to the generous and deeply knowledgeable Cathryn M. Oakley, David C. Stacy and Andrea Levario at HRC, Richard Burns and Jennifer C. Pizer at Lambda, Masen Davis at Freedom for All Americans, Reverend Stan J. Sloan at Family Equality, Amit Paley at The Trevor Project, and Jason Rosenberg at ACT UP NY.

I am lucky to work with Keith Hallworth, who brings his care, kindness, and extraordinary dedication to everything he does.

My deep appreciation to team Harper—Nick Davies, Tom Hopke, Beth Neelman Silfin, Dorian Randall, and John Jusino. This book is all the better for their belief and efforts.

I am so thankful for the dynamic Callie Schweitzer and grateful to be the beneficiary of her passion and creativity.

Thank you to my generous and keen early readers— Ali Winter, Andy Snyder, Dana Golub, Matthew Puccini, and Lea Carpenter.

Most especially, every day I give thanks to the incredible team of doctors and nurses at UCSF Medical Center Neonatal Intensive Care Unit who saved our son's life and, over his three-month stay, saved mine too.

About the Author

RICHIE JACKSON is an award-winning Broadway, television, and film producer who most recently produced the Tony Award–nominated *Harvey Fierstein's Torch Song* on Broadway. He was the executive producer of Showtime's *Nurse Jackie* (the Emmy and Golden Globe nominee for Best Comedy Series) for seven seasons and the co-executive producer of the film *Shortbus*, written and directed by John Cameron Mitchell. As an alumnus of New York University's Tisch School of the Arts, he endowed a fellowship program, the Richie Jackson Artist Fellowship, at his alma mater in 2015 to assist graduates in the transition from academia to a lifelong career in the arts. He and his husband, Jordan Roth, were honored with The Trevor Project's 2016 Trevor Hero Award. They live in New York City with their two sons.

A PORTION OF the proceeds from the sale of this book will be donated to The Trevor Project.

The Trevor Project is the world's largest suicide-prevention and crisis-intervention organization for LGBTQ (lesbian, gay, bisexual, transgender, queer, and questioning) youth. The organization works to save young lives by providing support through free and confidential suicide-prevention and crisis-intervention programs on platforms where young people spend their time. The Trevor Project offers a 24/7 phone lifeline, chat, and text, and will soon be integrated with social media platforms. The organization also runs Trevor-Space, the world's largest safe-space social networking site for LGBTQ youth, and operates innovative education, research, and advocacy programs.

IF YOU OR someone you know is feeling hopeless or suicidal, contact the 24/7 Trevor Project's TrevorLifeline at 1-866-488-7386. Counseling is also available 24/7/365 via chat at TheTrevorProject.org/Help, or by texting 678–678.